Rub up:
Musings of a Navy Corpsman

Rub up: Musings of a Navy Corpsman

A Novel

Mitchell J. Rycus

iUniverse, Inc.
New York Lincoln Shanghai

Rub up: Musings of a Navy Corpsman

Copyright © 2007 by Mitchell J. Rycus

All rights reserved. No part of this book may be used or reproduced by any means, graphic, electronic, or mechanical, including photocopying, recording, taping or by any information storage retrieval system without the written permission of the publisher except in the case of brief quotations embodied in critical articles and reviews.

iUniverse books may be ordered through booksellers or by contacting:

iUniverse
2021 Pine Lake Road, Suite 100
Lincoln, NE 68512
www.iuniverse.com
1-800-Authors (1-800-288-4677)

Because of the dynamic nature of the Internet, any Web addresses or links contained in this book may have changed since publication and may no longer be valid.

This is a work of fiction. All of the characters, names, incidents, organizations, and dialogue in this novel are either the products of the author's imagination or are used fictitiously.

ISBN: 978-0-595-43323-0 (pbk)
ISBN: 978-0-595-87662-4 (ebk)

Printed in the United States of America

This book is lovingly dedicated to my wife, Carole; my daughter, Lisa; and my son, Peter—to let them know that changing careers is never *not* an option.

Heart and Soul
from the Paramount Short Subject A SONG IS BORN
Words by Frank Loesser
Music by Hoagy Carmichael
Copyright (c) 1938 (Renewed 1965) by Famous Music LLC
International Copyright Secured All Rights Reserved

Prologue

BLACK TOOTH

He was missing a tooth on the upper right side of his jaw. When he smiled or grinned we could see a big, black hole there, and so we called him Black Tooth. He had an ancient look to him—a face that came out of the history books from every country where fighting was endemic. It was the leathery face of a crude, backwater soldier who had been conscripted from the farms or the urban slums but had stayed in the military after the war because that was the only thing he knew how to do. In fact, the military was the only place he was capable of getting a job anymore. He looked like he always needed a shave and was slightly—sometimes more than slightly—wasted or hungover. He was an alcoholic who always had a painful, hungry look on his face while he was sober and waiting to go on his next bender. If you saw him coming out of a dark alley, he would give you quite a start, even if he was in uniform. His dark, unshaven complexion; short, squatty frame; bowed legs; and unsteady gait presented a very scary picture, indeed. And if he spoke to you his deep gravelly voice alone would almost knock you over.

Yet Bill Jensen—or Wild Bill—was a gentle soul with that alcoholic's sense of humor that ingratiated him to everyone around. You couldn't help but smile through his homespun stories about whores or girlfriends—he rarely distinguished between the two, and most were probably fictitious anyway—and all the wild drunken exploits he had while on liberty. In fact that's how he came by the nickname Wild Bill. He never went on liberty with anybody, or maybe it was that nobody would go with him. Either way, he would always somehow make it back to the ship, sometimes carried by sailors who knew him, all messed up and as ugly and foreboding as ever.

He was only a seaman first—a deck ape—even though he had been in the Navy forever. He was probably only in his thirties, but he looked like he could have been anywhere from fifty to seventy years old, depending how hungover he was. His favorite stories were about his family. It might seem hard to believe just looking at him that someone somewhere might have cared or still cared about him, but he did have a family. In particular, he frequently talked about a young nephew who was living down South. I'm not sure if it was a sister's or a brother's son, but Black Tooth did seem to enjoy the kid. One of his favorite stories about his nephew—I don't think he ever referred to him as anything but "my nephew"—involved the kid starting to shave in his late teens.

Black Tooth would often tell this story to us while watching the younger sailors—or younger-looking sailors like me—shave. He would snicker and make fun of the fact that our faces were so much smoother than his own. Black Tooth's face looked like Popeye's archrival Bluto after a bad day of having it out with the one-eyed sailor. In his smoker's raspy alcoholic voice, Black Tooth would say to us, "Your face is just like my nephew's—smooth as a baby's ass. When I tell my nephew that his face is like a baby's ass he says to me, 'just rub up, Uncle Bill. See, it's not that smooth; just rub up.'" And Black Tooth would take his hand and rub up on his cheek where it sounded like he was rubbing sandpaper. He would chuckle and we would all smile, of course, and make nasty comments about how ugly old Black Tooth was and how nobody would ever want to look like him. But for his nephew, rubbing his own cheek like that and feeling the hint of facial hair was the promise of good things to come.

And I guess that's what life is all about—the promise of things to come, hope for the future and whatever promise of good things the future might bring—including a future of something as mundane as the ability to grow a beard. For Black Tooth, good things was getting a shot of cough medicine from me—elixir of terpin hydrate, which consisted mostly of 95 percent ethyl alcohol. He would come into sick bay with a fisted hand in front of his mouth, faking discomfort and then he would sputter, "(cough, cough …) Hey Doc, you got something for this?" I would give him a shot—sometimes a double—and he would leave with a smile on his homely, weathered face, his black tooth staring at me. And you could see in his eyes: "rub up, Uncle Bill; just rub up."

Chapter 1

1950—MICHAEL RABIN

"Rub up." I've been saying those two words in my head every morning for almost fifty years now. Whenever I look in the mirror while I'm shaving, I think, "Rub up, Uncle Bill," and smile. It makes me just a little more optimistic about this fucked up world we all live in. I remember how excited I was when I first started shaving. I think I was around seventeen and knew that I really didn't need to shave then, at least not every day. But it was a coming-of-age thing, even though at seventeen I still looked like I was fourteen. I was running around with an older crowd of guys, and they all shaved—so I shaved, too.

However, my grandfather, whose original name was Tzvi Rabinovich, never shaved. He was born sometime in the last half of the nineteenth century and lived in a Russian shtetl called Stolptsy. It was mostly a Jewish village—not unlike Anatevka, from *Fiddler on the Roof*—located in an area of Russia called Minsk Gubernia, or Minsk County in modern terms. Reb Rabinovich was the son of a rabbi (which, incidentally, is what Rabinovich means) and wore a handsome beard that was not to be shaved under Halachah (Jewish law). So when the Cossacks publicly cut off his beard in the village center in the early 1900s to show their contempt for Jews and to humiliate a prominent member of the Jewish community, Reb Rabinovich decided it was time to take his family and leave his home in Stolptsy for America. Once he left Russia, he never again shaved his beard. He wore it proudly and neatly trimmed until he died of old age at the Jewish Old Folks Home on Petoskey Street in Detroit.

I was born and raised in Detroit, Michigan, the only child of what was considered to be middle-class Jewish parents living in a Jewish neighborhood. Until high school, I attended schools that were primarily populated with Jewish kids. In addition, I had to go to Hebrew school from the time I was five until shortly after my bar mitzvah at thirteen. If my grandfather had his way, I would have gone on to the Yeshiva University in New York to become a rabbi—but being a rabbi was not for me. "Zadie, I love you very much, but I don't want to be a rabbi—I just want to be like all the other kids, okay?" was one of the hardest things for me to say to my zadie when I was just thirteen years old. The years that followed are filled with many happy, and almost as many sad memories, but some of the most influential years of my life occurred during the brief three year, nine month and eleven day period that I spent in the navy between 1950 and 1954, and that's what most of this story is about. I'm retired now after finishing a thirty-seven-year career as a math and science teacher in the public school system. This is somewhat interesting in itself because I never liked school; in fact, I never liked any kind of formally organized activity that required self-control and discipline.

I went to high school at Cass Tech—not Central like most of the other Jewish kids from the neighborhood. Cass Tech was a city wide school specializing in science and art whereas Central was the local neighborhood high school. I was enrolled in the art program, not just because I liked to draw but because I knew that I could go off by myself and draw without any faculty supervision or classmate distractions. Once I got my assignment, like drawing corridors to learn perspective, I frequently just kept on drawing into the next class period. I knew that technically I was marked down as skipping the next class, but that never really bothered me. I liked art classes where I could draw or paint, and I liked science classes like photographic chemistry. As for the other courses I had to take, such as English and social studies, I would just daydream through them or skip them entirely. I remember staring out the window one rainy, fall day when I heard my teacher say in a facetious voice, "Michael Rabin, are you sleeping or just dreaming?"

I looked up and saw that she was smirking. "I'm just thinking," I answered with no affect. Some of the kids giggled, which embarrassed me and made me feel like I didn't belong in the class.

Daydreaming in class didn't impact my grades because I had the ability to easily recall things I had heard or read. I had little trouble passing exams in those boring courses; I just remembered the stuff that I heard and used it to answer the exam questions. I thought I was cheating by just memorizing stuff and not figuring out the answers. I never told anyone how I felt, but as far as I was concerned, I was just faking my way through school by repeating things I memorized. I did this until I was seventeen, when much to my parents' chagrin, I finally quit high school. I told my mother the news one afternoon while she was vacuuming the house. As she began to move the vacuum around angrily, she said in an agitated voice, "So you'll be a bum like your friends." Then she continued as her voice grew more heated, "You're not going to hang around the house all day, so you better get a job and start paying some rent." I think her tone was more of disappointment than anger. She really thought I could be an artist if I stayed in school. I left the house in tears because I thought I could be an artist, too, but I thought I could do it on my own, not in a school setting.

I ran around with a bunch of guys who were pretty much from the neighborhood. We all were dating girls from an older and less affluent Jewish neighborhood around Twelfth Street. Gang fights, minor hassles with the police, and general roughhousing was the rule. My relatives called us *trombeniks,* a Yiddish word meaning "bums" or worse. I had no motivation at that time to be anything other than an artist, but I knew that would require a lot more practice and skill than I currently had. As a high school dropout with no working experience as an artist, I could find only relatively low-skilled jobs like lamp repairman or busboy. Many of my friends also wanted to be skilled workers like radio technicians or other tradesmen, but they had jobs that offered them opportunities to work and learn their skill while on the job.

Growing up with all the excitement and apparent romance of World War II (at least according to the movies), I also had a strong desire to be in the military. Since I missed getting into the army during the war, I felt somehow cheated by never having gone into battle with a .30 caliber air-cooled machine gun blazing away (without burning my hands off!)—just like in those old movies. After I quit school, my relatives were worried that I would end up being killed like my Uncle Mikie. Whenever they heard anything bad about any of the kids I was running around with—like if someone was arrested for stealing or being a hooligan—they couldn't wait to tell my parents or my grandparents. One Sunday, in the fall of 1949 shortly after I quit school, I heard my Aunt Betty—dad's sister-in-law—tell my father, "Mike needs closer supervision. You have to be a lot stricter with him—otherwise he could wind up getting murdered just like Mikie did from those gangsters he hung around with." My Uncle Mikie, whom I supposedly looked like had been my father's closest friend, so Aunt Betty's comment really got to him and in some way changed our relationship. He became short-tempered with me like the time I asked for the car and he said, "You can't have the car tonight! I don't want you bumming around looking for trouble, so just keep your ass in the house or there'll be no car any other time."

He had never yelled at me like that before, and I loudly responded, "Bullshit!" He started toward me like he was going to hit me, but I ran out of the house and avoided further confrontation. I know he wouldn't have smacked me, but there was a sense of apprehension in his eyes like I had never seen before.

When the Korean War broke out in June of 1950, I finally made up my mind to enlist. Although my parents struggled to accept my going into the service and maybe into battle, I do think that they were a little relieved that I was finally going off somewhere where discipline and listening to authority were required. I knew my dad was especially nervous, although he tried not to show it. He had already lost one Michael, his brother, to hoodlum violence; he was not keen on losing another Michael, his only child, to war violence.

* * * *

It seems strange that I wanted to go into the military as a volunteer. I remember the stories my grandfather told me about his "military career." In a mix of Yiddish and English, he would ask, "Michael, did I ever show you the exercises we did in the Palace Guards?" Then he would give me a quick demonstration of some very comical-looking arm lifts while he pretended to be holding a rifle. It seems that while my Zadie Tzvi Rabinovich was in Russia, he was conscripted as a reserve soldier in the Russian Palace Guards, as were most of the Jewish men living in the Russian shtetls. The so-called Palace Guards, most of whom never saw a palace, would be mobilized to fight for the czar as cannon fodder whenever it was to the czar's political benefit to get rid of some more Jews. However, the civil unrest of the late nineteenth century and the peasant's revolt in 1905, which ultimately led to the historic Russian Revolution later in the century, gave rise to further widespread anti-Semitism. Anti-Semitism was now felt even out in the remote shtetls of Minsk Gubernia. Not wanting to have to care for a bunch of Jewish orphans—and as another method of getting rid of the Jews—Czar Nicholas II allowed Jews with four or more children to leave the country. However, the ones leaving couldn't take anything of monetary value with them; just the minimum amount of gold, jewelry, or currency necessary to book passage out of the country. The family would have to abandon their property and any possessions that they couldn't carry on their backs. My father, Zelig (soon to be Sidney), the "blessed one," was just two years old when the family left Russia in the middle of a bitterly cold winter in February of 1908.

* * * *

Even though I knew all this family history, I still tried to enlist in the military. I first tried the air force; I loved military aircraft and could name and draw most of the World War II planes. I had made paper and balsa wood models of all sorts of military craft—trucks, ships, and especially airplanes. But the air force wouldn't take me on account of what they claimed were my "flat feet." During the physical we had to walk around naked from one examining station to another. At the end of the process, they had us lift up one foot. If the sole was dirty all over, we were rejected for flat feet. I found out that being rejected for this condition was not unusual. Later that summer, someone told me that to pass the physical I should walk around arching my feet to keep the bottoms as clean as possible and the arches as dirty as possible. When I went in for my navy physical, I did just that—and it worked.

On a rainy, early fall day in 1950, when the leaves were just beginning to turn, I left Detroit for boot camp at the United States Naval Training Center in Great Lakes, Illinois. I was very excited on the train, going first to Chicago and then changing in Chicago to the North Shore Line for Great Lakes. I enjoyed the thought of "playing" sailor—I didn't think of being in the navy as a job—and the anticipation was thrilling. Learning how to fight and shoot those big navy guns you see in the movies on the battle ships really excited me. But after a couple of weeks the initial excitement wore off and the routine grind of drilling, classes, inspections, and all things military grew somewhat tiresome. I did enjoy some of the training, such as fire-fighting school, and I actually took pride in how much my company had progressed with its marching abilities. I liked the little cadence-calling rhymes we sang when we marched: "I don't know but I've been told, Eskimo pussy's mighty cold. Sound off ..."

I also realized for the first time, but definitely not for the last time, that quitting high school may not have been the smartest decision I ever made. It seems that all incoming recruits are given the rank of Seaman Recruit in boot camp, but some of the guys were designated as HSSRs, which stood for high school seaman recruits. It meant that they had graduated from high school. When they enlisted they were told that they would have better naval career choices and greater opportunities for more interesting ratings, such as sonarman. They would also get the better duty assignments and have the option of attending various training schools. The rest of us would probably be sent to sea to swab decks and do shit details. I was not one for swabbing decks, so I was a little concerned that the

HSSRs would get all the best assignments. I thought that the worst assignments would go to older high school dropouts like me, and to the seventeen-year-old kids who dropped out just for the purpose of joining the navy.

As it turned out, toward the end of boot camp, the navy made us take a battery of tests that were supposed to determine what ratings each of us were best suited for. We then met with a second-class petty officer, a personnelman, who went over our test results and asked what ratings we were interested in pursuing. We were told that ratings like boatswain's mate and boilerman required no schooling or special training, while other ratings required attending a navy school. To be eligible for attending a navy school, the sailor had to have high test scores and evidence of success in a school environment. Finally, some ratings were based on civilian-related experience. In these cases, a sailor could become a "striker," or someone who has some special training or skill and is willing to serve under a senior petty officer, almost like an apprentice.

During my meeting with the petty officer, I was told my scores and asked what I was interested in. I had no idea what the scores meant, so I first asked the personnelman how I did on the tests. Surprisingly, he told me that I had scored very high and that I could pretty much go to any school I wanted as a result. "Gee, I'd like to be an aviation photographer's mate," I said, envisioning myself flying around and taking pictures with specialized aerial cameras.

"There's no school for that," the petty officer said in a conciliatory voice. "If you want to strike for that rating, you'd have to get assigned to an aircraft carrier or naval air station. Once on board you should check with the aviation photographer's mate—if there is one—to see if he's taking any strikers. You'd have to convince him that you'd be good at it because of your experience and training."

He waited for that to sink in and then continued. "On the other hand, if you go to a school, you'll be guaranteed that rating and wouldn't have to worry about going to sea as a deck ape right after boot camp." Even knowing that I had never finished high school, he told me some of the schools I could go, such as sonar school or hospital corps school.

I was not keen on going to school, but the thought of going out to sea, taking a chance on being nothing more than a deck ape gave me some pause. "Well, what do you think would be best for me?" I asked. "I'm interested in seeing some action." I spoke like a true World War II kid who was raised on those great, patriotic war movies.

"Hospital corps school," he said without hesitation. "Best of all, they really dropped the course length; down to only eight weeks! And with any luck, after serving a year or less at a naval hospital, you could get into the marines as a fleet marine corpsman. In case you didn't know, the marines are part of the navy and corpsmen can serve in either branch." Now that sounded like what I wanted.

Much later I learned that fleet marine corpsmen were being killed off or wounded in action at a relatively high rate in Korea, and that was why the corps school course length had been cut to eight weeks. In addition, personnelmen were being pressured to get qualified sailors to sign up for corps school because corpsmen were desperately needed. Even when I learned this, I still looked forward to being a fleet marine corpsman. I thought that just because some other guys didn't want to be marines, or felt that going into a war zone was for suckers, there was no reason for me to feel that way. But I did wonder a little as to why they were having trouble getting "qualified" people and that they were taking me, a high school dropout, to go to corps school.

The last week of boot-camp I broke my thumb on a garbage detail—a duty assignment usually reserved for punishing bad behavior. It was over the Christmas weekend and a week before I was to start corps school. Being placed on garbage detail with the four other Jewish recruits in my company over Christmas weekend seemed to us to be more than just a coincidence. Nobody from our company was given permission to go home that weekend and it seemed odd that only the Jewish guys were singled out for a shit-detail. We had heard expressions like, "Christ killer," around that time so we knew what it was all about. That incident turned out to be the first of a number of anti-Semitic incidents that I experienced in the navy.

My broken thumb didn't prevent me from graduating boot camp on time. So, after three months of boot camp, I got my shipping orders to report across the road to Great Lakes Hospital and attend corps school. I wasn't much for formal schooling and hoped I could last the eight weeks without getting into serious trouble—or worse, getting thrown out and sent to sea as a deck ape. But the chance to get my combat experience as a fleet marine corpsman was an even greater incentive to survive corps school.

* * * *

A couple of weeks after starting school I had a life awakening experience at the hospital that caused me to think a little more seriously about my fighting ambitions. I was at the hospital to get my short hand cast removed when a marine who was injured in Korea was wheeled in on a gurney to have his leg cast changed. One of the corpsmen on duty knew that I had recently started corps school and asked me to wait until they took care of the marine. Recognizing I was in corps school, the corpsman offered me the chance to observe the changing of a leg cast, which I happily accepted. While the corpsmen prepared for the procedure, I talked with the injured marine. "So, how did you get your wound?" I asked him.

He was a young man, maybe nineteen or twenty, and he had a blank look in his eyes that I later learned many injured combat personnel had—and not because of the pain medication they were on. He stared through me into the distance but eventually spoke. "Our company was fighting gooks on some goddamned shithole of a hill," he said and then he paused, collecting his thoughts. Still staring away and with obvious pain in his eyes he continued, "I got blasted by a fuckin' mortar shell, and it tore my leg open." He went on to describe that part of Korea as a cold, barren, ugly place, with very little around to justify all the trouble they were having taking it. He was treated at a MASH unit, flown back to San Diego for more surgery and treatments, and ended up at Great Lakes, where he would receive long-term treatment and rehab before being discharged.

When the corpsmen were ready, the doctor came in and removed the marine's cast with a vibrating cast cutter that sounded like a buzz saw. When the cast was removed I saw his leg, or what was left of his leg. Like raw meat attached to the bone, it was a mangled mass of tissue, with green-stained gauze drains coming out of the infected wounds. As I wondered why they didn't just cut his leg off, I got dizzy and almost passed out. One of the corpsman noticed me looking very pale and quickly got me out of the room.

When they came to remove my cast later, they told me not to worry; getting queasy was not unusual for beginners. They said that once I graduated corps school and was sent to a hospital, I would quickly get used to seeing all kinds of gory things—which I wasn't sure I wanted to get used to! I asked the corpsman about the marine. "Why don't you just cut off his leg and give him a wooden leg?"

"Eventually we may have to do that," the corpsman said, "but if there's any chance of saving his leg, especially the knee, the kid was better off. His own leg, even if it's gimpy, is better in the long run than any manufactured leg."

The day rested heavy on me. I kept thinking about getting dizzy in the cast room and the blank stare of the marine. It didn't change my mind about wanting to be a marine corpsman, but I realized that it wasn't going to be as much fun as I thought it would be—not because I thought that I would get hurt, but because I would have to treat guys like that injured marine in the field. I would have to do all I could to save a leg or an arm or a life. That was a heavy responsibility, and it didn't seem like "fun" would play any part in it. I got my cast removed and returned to school with a new attitude and a healthier sense of what might be expected of me once I graduated and got into the fleet marines.

* * * *

My desire to get into combat still seemed strange to me when I recalled once again how my family felt about going to war. They told me that when World War I broke out the family was worried that my dad's brother, Uncle Jack, might have to go into the army, even though my uncle was still in high school. But the war in Europe ended, so Uncle Jack stayed home, graduated from high school, and worked with my Zadie Tzvi in the poultry store. Some of my dad's sister's high school friends did go off to war, though; one was killed in action, which my Aunt Faye never forgot. After that she was always a staunch pacifist, even during World War II. Strange as it may seem, my family's strong negative feelings about going into the military and into combat had little impact on my behavior and choices at this point in my life.

I anxiously started corps school with the concern that I wouldn't be able to stick with it, do all the work that might be required of me, and keep from getting bored. As it turned out, I really enjoyed the corps school experience. I met a whole new breed of sailor, many of whom had attended college or even finished premed programs. It was quite a revelation to find people to talk to that were more interesting than most of the folks I grew up with in Detroit. During meals and in the evening when we weren't talking about our class work these guys talked about reading books and listening to the news about the war. "Do you think Truman will fire MacArthur for wanting to take on China?" one of my fellow students asked me during dinner.

I wasn't that familiar with the whole controversy and even so I thought it was certainly not my place to question that level of authority. "I don't know. I think going to war with China would be stupid, but that's their decision" I said. Others joined in on the discussion calling MacArthur everything from an arrogant asshole to an American hero. They really seemed interested in what was going on in the world. They also were concerned with what our leaders were going to do and what impact it might have on them, the country, and their future—in other words, they behaved like adults. It was contagious in the sense that I also wanted to talk like them and take a greater interest in my job. My job—I was no longer *playing* sailor—was now something more to me than just a way to become a combat marine. I was growing up and recognizing the need for more adult behavior—but occasionally I stumbled.

Early on in corps school, I received a letter from a boot camp buddy who told me that after boot camp he went to Seattle, Washington, where he met up with five of his future shipmates, all of them recent boot camp graduates. They were on their way to Bremerton, Washington, and the Puget Sound Naval Shipyard to catch their ship—an aircraft carrier. He went on to tell me that they went out and got wasted and all got tattoos. He drew me a picture of his; it looked like an eagle wrapped in a banner that had USN spelled on it, and there was an anchor located behind the eagle. How cool, I thought—these guys were finally real sailors.

In corps school, sailors had it made because we had every weekend off to go into town, go home, or do what we wanted to. But we were still expected to study over the weekends because there was a lot of material that we had to learn. On the weekend after I got my buddy's letter, I didn't feel the need to study, so I took a train into Milwaukee, Wisconsin. There on a bright and cold day in January, I located a well-known tattoo artist—at least one well-known to sailors. I scanned over his artistry displayed on the walls for a naval design similar to the one my friend drew for me. There were many to choose from, but I found one that had a larger eagle with his banner ending in a fish tail and there were stars on either side of the eagle's head. I thought it looked just as cool as my buddy's— maybe even cooler. Stone-cold sober, I told the artist, "Let's get that one."

The artist shaved my left forearm, which is where my friend had his tattoo. After swabbing the area down with alcohol and covering it with Vaseline (at least I think it was Vaseline), he placed a clear plastic template on my greasy arm with the outline of my chosen artwork formed from tiny holes drilled through the plastic. He poured some graphite or some other black powder on the template and then he removed it, and the outline of the tattoo stood out clearly. I was thrilled that I was having this done when he started in with the electric vibrating needles. I could not believe the initial pain; like a bolt of electricity shot through my arm. I was almost crying from the pain and I wanted to scream for him to stop! All I could think was, "What kind of schmuck am I for even thinking about doing this goyishe thing!" I sort of knew that my family would not appreciate my getting tattooed because Jews just didn't do that kind of body disfiguring. After a few minutes, though, my arm became completely numb, and as I relaxed, I actually enjoyed watching the artist work. He was good. He knew his craft well and told me, "I'm glad you're not drunk cause I never tattoo drunken sailors. Wouldn't be right to do this to someone who wasn't sure they knew what they're doing," he said. His voice was soft and steady, and it seemed he was just saying that to keep me calm and to take my mind off of the pain because he was concentrating very hard on his work. I was pleased to know that he had some scruples about his work and I was just young enough to believe him.

I spent the rest of the day and evening in Milwaukee. I met another sailor from the base at a drugstore where we struck up a conversation. He was attending another school there and asked what brought me into town and I told him I came in to get tattooed. We seemed to hit it off well, so we went together to a local USO and had dinner with some nice Wisconsin girls. "Mike came in to get tattooed today," my new friend told the girls just to get a conversation going.

One of the girls seemed all excited about my new tattoo and asked, "Can you show it to us? What's a new tattoo look like? Does it sorta have to develop like a photograph?"

I nervously explained the process because I didn't want to gross them out, "No, uh ..., they do it with ink and uh ..., like using needles they draw it under your skin. It's still pretty bloody now, but that will heal in a day or two. Are you sure you still want to see it?" I said, as I slowly removed the gauze, and with oohs and ahs, they commented on the bright reds, blues, and greens and the touch of yellow coloring that augmented the mostly black design. I had to explain what it was—an eagle over an anchor—but they did seem impressed.

*   *   *   *

The next day I woke up and removed the bandage to see a huge, bloody brown scab—which I had expected to find. I showed off my new, scabby tattoo to some of my fellow classmates later that day. Most were simply bored, but more than one told me I was stupid for doing it. "Don't you know you could get all kinds of blood-transmitted diseases like hepatitis?" a friend said to me. He shook his head and continued. "Worst of all, you may not know for as many as seventy years whether or not you're safe from leprosy." I was embarrassed and a little ashamed, but after a couple more days of razzing, my friends just ignored the whole thing. However, Ben Brailey—a rotund, jovial friend from the East—continued to tease me.

"Mike," Ben whispered to me in class, "I'm thinking about getting an eye tattooed in the middle of my forehead. What do you think about that?" Then later he murmured, "Hey, how about bumblebees coming out of my belly button?" Still later that day, he said, "I think I'll get a tattoo of an *M* on each cheek of my ass so when I bend over it spells *MOM*. What do you think of that? And if I stand on my head it will spell *WOW!* Do you like that one?" I knew it was all good-natured kidding, but I got the idea that Ben and the others were telling me

I had acted childishly. Although the tattoo might not prove fatal, it would affect me for the rest of my life—a fact that became clear to me when I went home the following weekend to see a movie with my girlfriend and our old gang.

My friends picked me up at the train station, and we went directly downtown to see *King Solomon's Mines* at the Palms Theater. It had started to snow when we went out for a snack after the movie, and the snow-covered streets kept me from getting home till after midnight. My parents had been expecting me and were asleep when I came in, or rather I thought they were, but they were more than likely awake to make sure I came home safely. Sunday morning I woke up to the smell of coffee and imagined the bagels and lox I knew were waiting for me. Soon my dad came into the bedroom to see if I was awake. He asked, "Well are you ready for a good breakfast? How about a couple of your favorite salty bagels with lox? I got that good Muenster cheese you like; would you like a couple of eggs too?"

I said, "Eggs sound real good to me, dad."

My father then added, "We should leave for the train before eleven so you better get up now, okay?"

We then started talking a little about my date, but my new tattoo was on my mind and I said, "Hey Pa! Take a look at this." I proudly displayed my colorfully tattooed forearm.

Shocked, my father stared in utter disbelief then he yelled at me. "What's this? You did this to yourself? You didn't even need the Nazis to do it to you—you had to do it yourself? Are you crazy? You're not my son; you're not my boy, Michael." He started to leave the room, then turned and angrily said, "And another thing, don't ever show it to your mother."

When he turned around again and slowly walked out the bedroom door just shaking his head from side to side I felt sick to my stomach and I never felt so ashamed in my life. I knew that Jews didn't get tattoos, but I found out later that it was actually a sin for Jews to get tattoos; it was considered a mutilation of one's body. That was one of the reasons why the Nazis tattooed the Jews in the concentration camps—it was one more way to humiliate them. My father and I didn't speak much more that cloudy winter day, and the car was filled with a chilly silence when we left for the train station. There was little traffic that Sunday morning and nothing much on the car radio to listen to as we drove toward downtown. The silence was almost deafening; I wanted to talk but I couldn't think of anything to say. My father did kiss me good-bye; I knew I was not forgiven, but I also knew I was still loved. Pretending to sleep on the train, I cried silently almost all the way back to Great Lakes.

* * * *

I loved the fast pace of the school and there were lots of things to memorize—anatomy, medical terms, first aid, field procedures—all of which came easy to me. Our instructors were nurses and HM1s—first-class petty officers. Occasionally a chief corpsman would surface briefly for specific tasks such as record keeping and shot charts, but most of the time the same nurse did the teaching. One day our anatomy and physiology instructor, an HM1, announced at the end of class, "There are 206 bones in the human body—tomorrow's your test on them." He passed out sheets of paper showing a skeleton in a number of different views and spaces on the bones for us to write in their names. He said, "For a study guide you should fill in the blanks on these handouts using your text book. For tomorrow's exam I'll give you a blank copy to fill in." I had no problem memorizing the names of the bones, and after just a couple of hours studying my text and practicing filling in the blanks, I felt confident about the upcoming bones test. I noticed later in the day in our sleeping quarters that most of my classmates were still poring over their textbooks, filling in chart after chart and apparently many had been studying for hours.

"Hey Rabin, you better study this shit or you'll flunk the test tomorrow and get sent down a class," my friend Ben warned me that evening. Corps school was different than civilian schools in that students couldn't flunk out even if they wanted to. They would have to keep repeating whatever course they failed, even if it meant going into a later graduating class. Rumor had it that if a student was put into later graduating classes more than five times, he or she would be dishonorably discharged, but I don't think that was true. Once again, I had that guilty feeling that I was faking it—not really learning, just memorizing—so I after Ben's warning I pretended to study longer and stared at another blank chart for a while before slowly and carefully filling it in. I didn't want my classmates to find out that I memorized it already for fear that they would accuse me of cheating. The next day I breezed through the exam and got all 206 bones right. Ben told me I aced it because of his prodding me to study a little harder.

Despite some of my concerns about my own learning methods, corps school did have its lighter moments. We all teased each other about going into the fleet marines. I never told anyone that being a fleet marine was my goal, as only "idiots" went voluntarily into the marines. At school we heard all sorts of horror stories from the older and "wiser" students. One Saturday morning in our common area a student who had been there a whole two weeks longer than us told us,

"Hey, you guys that are headed to Korea. Did you know that the North Koreans had figured out that if they killed a corpsman, then they had also killed ten marines? They figured this was because a corpsman should save ten lives before he himself was taken out." This seasoned pro also went on to tell us, "You know we're classified as noncombatants, so we aren't issued weapons. So I'm telling you, that as soon as you enter your first combat zone, grab a weapon off of any dead body, whether it's an enemy's body or one of our own."

We pondered this for a while when this older guy went on, "You know they give you combat helmets with the big red crosses that are circled in white, and according to the Geneva Convention's rules of warfare, the enemy's supposed to respect the cross as a sign of our noncombatant status. But that first aid symbol on your helmet gives the gooks a perfect target to take aim at. So as soon as you could—get another helmet, preferably off the same body from which you get your weapon."

I didn't know how true any of that stuff he told us was, but even though we acted like it was no big deal to get a weapon off of a dead combatant I'm certain that our attitude was mostly whistling-in-the-dark behavior. Take the singing of our theme song to the tune of "My Bonnie Lies Over the Ocean":

> Take down the blue star flag, mother,
> Put up the gold one instead.
> Your son is a fleet marine corpsman,
> In twenty-one days he'll be dead.
>
> So dead, so dead,
> With twenty-one holes in his head, his head.
> So dead, so dead,
> With twenty-one holes in his head.

Later I learned that other military units had similar so-called theme songs, many of which were made up during World War II or even before. At first you think the song is funny, or maybe even cute, but our civilian friends would hear it and think that we were being crass. The Korean War was not important to civilians in the same way that World War II was. Nobody at home was suffering; there was no rationing or shortages, no air raid drills—with the exception of atom bomb drills in the schools—and worst of all, the war was referred to as a "police action." People didn't think we were in a real war where an enemy might actually attack the country. As a result, the public didn't want to be bothered hearing about deaths, maiming, and injuries. They had just recently come out of World War II and were tired of war. Now was the time to get rich and get a better life, which at that time meant getting things like cars and houses and forgetting about war. Hearing songs about sailors getting killed in action in three weeks made them uncomfortable. In any event, it was strange for us in the service to be kidding ourselves about going off to battle, which was very likely to happen, and for the rest of the country to not want any part of that whole "war" thing.

*   *   *   *

I graduated from corps school with a good overall grade of 3.8 out of a possible 4.0, even though I thought I had cheated my way through by memorizing most everything. My parents were delighted that I had finally graduated from some kind of school. It was the end of February, and I had a week to report to Chelsea Naval Hospital outside of Boston, Massachusetts. I planned to stay in Detroit for most of the week and then take the train to Boston, but the mild weather inspired my father and mother to decide to take a few days off and drive me there. That way they'd have some vacation time together coming back. I also think my dad was a little relieved that I was going to the East Coast and not the West Coast, where in his perception the war was right offshore. We stopped in Buffalo, New York, the first night and stayed in a Boston hotel the second night. The next day my parents drove me around the city to show me some of the places, like the Boston Common that they thought I would enjoy seeing. I was anxious to get started at my new duty station and wanted to go right up to the hospital, but I didn't want to disappoint my folks by rushing them. I think they would have thought I didn't want to spend more time with them so I acted like I was very appreciative of their showing me around Boston.

Boston looked like an interesting place, smaller than Detroit but more interesting looking streets and buildings. I saw lots of sailors walking around the downtown area of the city and that made me feel comfortable about being there. But I had heard that there were signs in some of the parks that said, "Dogs and Sailors not Allowed." Later in the day they drove me through the front gate of Chelsea up to the main hospital entrance. Chelsea Naval Base was a large military complex spread out over almost 100 acres. Some of the buildings dated back to the mid-1800s, even before the Civil War. The hospital grounds were located at the foot of the Mystic River Bridge, and on a good day when the smoke and fog had cleared off the river you could see the famous Charleston Naval shipyard where the USS Constitution (Old Ironsides) was docked. A lot of newer wooden buildings had been added among the older brick buildings during World War II, which gave the base a mixed, eclectic architecture.

We looked at the hospital facility from the outside for a while, and then they both hugged and kissed me. Mom said, "Be sure to write and let us know if you need anything, and take care of yourself, and … and be good."

Dad simply said in a stern voice, "Stay out of trouble." I watched them drive off, picked up my seabag and went in.

I was going on nineteen and I was a hospitalman apprentice, and if I behaved, I would soon be a hospitalman first. I knew that I had to stay at Chelsea Naval at least until I made hospitalman, but right after that I would start volunteering for the fleet marines. This was what I looked forward to—the promise of seeing some military action. What I didn't know was that at Chelsea Naval I was about to meet different kinds of people—people like I had never met before. Officers, enlisted men, and civilians from different worlds and cultures were about to completely change the way I thought about myself and even how I behaved.

It's a good thing that most military personnel are young and easily taken in by the romance of battle; if they weren't, civilized countries would never be able to find enough people to wage war. I had heard sentiments like this before from returning World War II vets, but walking into a hospital filled with war casualties gave me an understanding of these thoughts for the first time.

CHAPTER 2

1951—GRADY DUMONT

When they brought Major Grady Dumont into Chelsea Naval Hospital during the spring of 1951, he was closer to being dead than he was to being alive. He had just experienced a massive heart attack and was totally out of it—partly because he had passed out, and partly because of the medication he was given. His skin was a blue-gray color and looked clammy, and his normally ruddy complexion had turned to splotchy patches of pink. We put him in a private room on the Sick Officer Quarters (SOQ) ward and positioned an oxygen tent, with its see-through plastic window, over his head and chest. From what I was told, he had been brought in by ambulance all the way from somewhere around Concord, Massachusetts, a distance of over eighteen miles. The area around Concord was mostly rural at that time and the major's house and land were near Walden Pond, so it took a lot longer, probably close to an hour, to drive him here.

In any case, the doctors put him on a treatment of oxygen inhalation therapy, blood thinners, painkillers, and bed rest. Bypass surgery and all the other modern diagnostic and curative choices that are available to heart patients today didn't exist in the early 1950s. An EKG confirmed the diagnosis of a heart attack, so we more or less just let the major rest and waited for him to recover. The fact that the long ambulance drive in to Chelsea didn't kill him gave the doctors hope that he might recover.

When a corpsman graduates and is assigned to a hospital, he comes in with the rank of HA (hospitalman apprentice) and displays two white stripes on the sleeve of his navy blue jumper with a caduceus above them. His, or her—many WAVES were trained as corpsmen—first assignment at a hospital was usually ward duty. For about six months, the new batch of ward corpsmen—affectionately called "bedpan jockeys"—would serve on a variety of wards—SOQ, an isolation ward, a post operation ward, and so on. After six months of ward duty, they might be assigned to a specialty duty such as lab tech or operating room (OR) technician. Normally corpsmen would spend a year at the hospital and if promoted to HM3 (hospital corpsman third class—the lowest-ranking petty officer), they would be eligible for a variety of new assignments. A choice assignment was independent sea duty—"independent" because no doctor would be permanently stationed onboard. As a result, the corpsman would treat sick and injured personnel independent of a doctor's guidance. Corpsmen on independent duty could serve at sea on a small ship like a destroyer, or they could serve on land at a remote overseas facility. Other assignments might include being stationed on a large ship like an aircraft carrier that actually had a field hospital onboard. In fact, corpsmen would be sent wherever the navy needed them— including my choice, the fleet marines in Korea. Even before the year of hospital duty is up, the corpsman might earn his HN (hospitalman first) rank and be asked to volunteer for the fleet marines. This could occur as early as just four or five months into his first hospital assignment, but that would be rare. My first assignment at Chelsea was SOQ.

* * * *

Major Dumont started to come around the next day; we had him "tubed up" with fluids in glass bottles hanging from the IV stand. On the nightstand next to his bed we placed all the things that he had in his pockets when they brought him in: wallet, money, cigarettes, lighter, and other items typically found in men's pockets. I had peeked in to see if he was awake so I could introduce myself, when I saw through the plastic window in the oxygen tent that he was awake and looking very groggy. He must have reached over to his nightstand because he had a cigarette in his mouth and his Zippo lighter in his hand, ready to flip it open and strike it. I quickly but gently reached under the tent. I didn't shout or rush him, for fear of giving him another heart attack, but quietly took the lighter out from under the tent and just as gently took the cigarette out of his mouth. I purposely had a big smile on my face as I said, "Welcome to Chelsea Naval, sir. I'm Hospitalman Apprentice Mike Rabin, the ward corpsman." He looked slightly dazed and a little confused but nodded assent and laid back and closed his eyes. I found the ward nurse, who rushed into his room and looked around for any other dangerous items, such as matches. While she was there, she checked the major's pulse. He sensed her touch on his wrist and opened his eyes. For the first time I was struck by the intensity of life in his steel-gray eyes. They were filled with a twinkle that indicated intelligence, a sense of humor, and with a wink to me, an awareness of just how close he had come to blowing himself up.

Grady Dumont was probably in his fifties and was a retired Marine Corps major, a mustang who came up through the enlisted ranks during World War II and retired after thirty or more years of service. He had been living in the countryside, where I gathered he was more than content to be out on a few acres of land enjoying his life. Then the heart attack hit him. I don't know who found him out there or how he got to the ambulance. I'm not even sure if he was living alone. I don't ever remember a wife or housemate visiting him, although he did have a sizable number of visitors over the course of his stay. He was originally from the South—possibly Louisiana—and talked with a slow and gentle southern drawl. He was a big man—not fat—but big in size and girth. He was good-humored and smiled a lot, but when he got serious you could almost see his mind working. After analyzing the issues being discussed, he would make thoughtful, well-reasoned responses. He acted that way when his doctor would discuss his prognosis and tell him what he had to do once he returned home. The doctor told him how often he wanted to examine him, how frequently he would have EKGs, and what meds he would be taking. Grady would listen intently. One time I heard him ask, "Will I be taking these pills for the rest of my life? And when can I get back to doing my housework? I need to start splitting logs for winter now."

* * * *

As Major Dumont healed and became more mobile, he would often advise me on my noticeably carefree and immature behavior. As a teenaged sailor, I was very much undisciplined and headed for trouble, and the major knew it. I'm sure he probably saw in me a little of himself when he was a young marine. That doesn't mean I was negligent toward the patients or that I didn't take my work seriously; it just meant that I pulled childish stunts like sneaking off the base to go drinking with a fake ID. It was the kind of behavior that wasn't always smart and was frequently risky. One time my buddy and I got caught by the Shore Patrol (SP) and were cited for being "out of uniform." We were at the amusement park on Revere Beach, trying to look cool for the teenage girls in the park. We were wearing our white hats incorrectly tilted on the backs of our heads—like the sailors we saw in the movies—and we had the cuffs of our jumpers rolled up, not down over our wrists and properly buttoned. If you were caught out of uniform in those days, the SPs would just stop you and take away your liberty pass so that you had to return to your base immediately. Later you would have to appear before a (disciplinary) captain's mast.

Grady found out about my run in with the SPs. I can still see the broad smile on his face as he spoke in his soft southern accent: "Haven't you got the brains that God gave a pissy-ant?" He went on to point out that losing my liberty and having a captain's mast on my record was not worth the short-term, if any, benefit of trying to look cool for the ladies. Of course he made sense, and he advised me in a way that was not berating or ridiculing. Even the "pissy-ant" remark wasn't meant to hurt or demean me. Grady was liked and respected by all the corpsmen on the ward. He treated us with dignity and understanding, and he was just plain fun to talk with and be around.

* * * *

Now it just so happened that at the same time Major Dumont was at Chelsea Naval Hospital, Second Lieutenant James Tibbits, United States Army, Retired, was also there being treated for one of his many ailments. Lieutenant Tibbits served in World War I, received a field commission during battle, and then reverted back to his sergeant rank when the war ended. However, in retirement he was allowed to use the highest rank held in service as long as it wasn't stripped from him for disciplinary reasons. Consequently, he was admitted to Chelsea Naval Hospital as a lieutenant, stayed in SOQ, and was treated for any of his long list of illnesses—military related or not. A tall, skinny guy in his sixties, Tibbits was quite spry for someone who claimed to be sick all the time. I think during this particular visit he was being treated for ulcers, but then again it could have been for hemorrhoids or some other gastrointestinal problem from one end of the alimentary canal to the other.

Tibbits had heard about the major and was anxious to meet him. Shortly after the major came out of his initial stupor and was able to receive visitors, Tibbits came bustling into his room, quickly introduced himself, and started to query the major before giving out his very opinionated advice. "Where're you gonna live now that you've had a hod-atak?" he asked in his pronounced New England twang. The major said, in a somewhat surprised manner, that he just planned on living in the countryside near Concord.

"Oh, no, no, no ... you can't do that," Tibbits said. "You've had a serious hod-atak, and you need to move into Bawston so you can be nearah to Chelsea."

"I don't think so," Major Dumont replied, still surprised that someone he doesn't really know could get so personal with him. "I kind of like my place in the country."

"No, no, you'll have to move into town here 'cause it will probably happen again. And then what would you do?" Tibbits asked.

The major said slowly, "Well ..., you could always just die."

Now he didn't say that flippantly just to get rid of Tibbits the boor; he said it after some reflection, just as when he talked with his doctor. And I realized that he really meant it. There I was, just a teenaged kid, and here was this man talking about dying and really meaning it—a man who had seen the face of death close-up, probably more than once from what I knew of his service record. Major Grady Dumont had come to terms with death and knew that at some point in his life he would really die. He refused to alter his way of life, which is what he held dear to him, simply because he might die a little sooner.

The major's remark reminded me of my only personal knowledge about a family's experience with death—the story of my Uncle Mikie. After Mikie graduated high school in 1921, the country was struggling with the effects of the Volstead Act, which for two years had prohibited the sale and consumption of alcohol in public places. However, economic times were good then, and people working in the entertainment business had it made, or so it seemed. Entertainers could do well if they had the requisite talent and were willing to work in speakeasies or the fancier illegal nightclubs. Along with floor shows and dancing, some of these clubs offered their guests the chance to drink alcohol and gamble. Mikie was cut out for show business; his dark complexioned good looks and dynamic personality seemed a perfect match for someone who wanted to be in the entertainment racket. Mikie could sing, dance, and tell jokes and would make an all around great host at any club. He had become acquainted with some people who were affiliated with the local entertainment business, but from the wrong side of the law. Some of Mikie's former high school friends were related to members of the Purple Gang—Detroit's infamous criminal organization. The gang of mostly Jewish mobsters was known for running booze across the Detroit River from Canada and ruthlessly getting rid of any competition through assassination. They were as vicious as the East Coast's Murder, Incorporated gang. In fact, the Purple Gang was frequently accused of being affiliated with Murder, Incorporated. In early 1922, they got Mikie an interview at a fancy night club called the Club Trocadero located on West Grand Boulevard. The club served illegal booze, but offered dancing and floor shows as well. Even though Mikie was only eighteen, his school records said he was nineteen and his vibrant personality, good looks, and entertainment skills were perfect for the job. According to my family, Uncle Mikie got a little too close to the vicious Purple Gang. So it came as no surprise to those watching Mikie's successful venture into show biz that in 1924, when my uncle was just twenty years old, he was accidentally shot and killed in a gang-related altercation with some hoods out of New Jersey. The shooters were never caught, and no one was ever charged with a crime.

The family was devastated, especially my father, who was inconsolable at the funeral and all during the week they sat shivah for Mikie. Dad had just graduated from high school and was looking forward to working with Mikie in their own club, which they had already planned to do. Mikie would put the show together and manage the entertainment, while Dad would handle the business end. Mikie could never handle the money side of the job; in fact, it was Dad who did all the business operations for the dance lessons that Mikie gave at the house. Dad set and collected the fees and made sure the money was safely put away in a 3% interest-bearing account at the American Loan and Savings bank on Cortland and Dexter. Uncle Mikie was the kind of person who never needed a lot of money—people would pick up his check or treat him to meals, movies, and whatever. So Mikie was surprised and delighted when my dad gave him ten dollars a week from Mikie's own dance lesson earnings to spend how he wanted. He had no idea he was making that kind of money just for teaching the latest dance steps to the girls and even some guys who wanted to be popular. But after Uncle Mikie was killed, Dad lost all interest in the business. I was told that my father lost his best friend who loved him, treated him with respect, and was a critical part of his life. It was during shivah that Dad, still sobbing every time he touched the cut tie he was required by Jewish custom to wear, decided that his firstborn son would be named Michael. He would do this to honor Uncle Mikie's name and to be certain that he, and everyone else, would remember Mikie forever. Given that kind of history, it was hard for me to envision death as ever being something you "could always just" do.

* * * *

The day Major Dumont left Chelsea, he dressed in his full Marine Corps uniform, ribbons and all. With his battle-hardened posture, he was quite the picture of military pride. Even though he had lost some weight—his uniform hung a little loosely around his frame—he looked great. Although I certainly respected him before, I must admit to having even more admiration after seeing him standing tall in his khakis and moving on. I reached out to shake his hand and then quickly withdrew, remembering that military etiquette dictated that an enlisted man (EM) should never reach out to shake hands with an officer; instead, he should wait and let the officer, if he wanted, reach out to him. I started to mumble, "I forgot the hand shake rule, and I ... and I ..."

The major pulled my hand back and shook it firmly. "Thanks, Mike, for the good care you've given me," he said. "You're going to be a damn good corpsman, and I know you'll have a successful military career. Good luck, Mike." He had that smile on his face and a telling look that said even though he had suffered a severe medical crisis and would in all likelihood not live as long as he might have expected, he was certainly going to conduct the rest of his life his way. He would live at his own pace, wherever in the world he wanted. And when the time came for him to die, he would probably be ready and accepting—if accepting death is really ever possible—since he had done it mostly on his own terms. I believe he was one of the wisest men I have ever known.

Major Grady Dumont, more than anyone I had met up to that time, convinced me that I should be a marine. He made me believe that being a marine would show that I was also a man capable of being in combat—just like the major and the other World War II vets. I think I just wanted to show everyone that I had grown up, and now I was brave enough to be a soldier. On the other hand, Grady also showed me that bravery could be demonstrated in ways other than combat. Bravery could be shown by your life choices and your ability to stay with those choices, no matter how scary they might turn out to be. By the same token, it could also mean not being afraid of having to do something else. For example, if I couldn't get into the marines or see action in combat, then I needed to recognize that I might just have to do what was expected of me and be brave about that, too. Even though I never did get into the marines, it was not as disappointing as I thought it would be. My parents never knew about my frequent voluntary attempts to be a fleet marine corpsman, but I'm sure their hopes and prayers were answered when I ended up not going to Korea.

It wasn't just men like Major Grady Dumont who made me rethink my image of who I was and what I wanted to be. Soon I would meet two women who would also have a significant impact on my idea of what defined a man. These women would also influence my behavior as to how I, as a man, should act toward women whether they are love interests or persons of authority.

Chapter 3

1951—SISTER MARIE THERESE AND ROSE DOMOKOS

Rowland Pelletier—he pronounced it "PEL-tzee-ai"—was almost a year older than me, had a noticeable French accent to reflect his hometown of Frenchville, Maine, was always excited, and was just a delight to be with. Rowle (pronounced "ROLL-ai") had graduated from hospital corps school a couple of weeks after I did and came to Chelsea Naval Hospital in the spring of 1951. We got to know each other over the summer and became close friends. We went on liberty together, drank together, roller-skated at Revere Beach together, picked up girls together, and broke all kinds of rules together.

Even though I was soon to turn nineteen, I still looked very young—sixteen on a good day—but a young WAVE corpsman helped me steal a blank birth certificate from the hospital maternity ward. I gave myself a fake name that I could easily remember and that would not catch me off guard if someone called me by my real name. I knew a kid in high school whose name was Mitch but whom everybody called Mike. I thought the name Mitchell would be believable even if someone heard me called Mike after they had seen my fake ID. So I chose Mitchell Ryan—Mitch Ryan sounded Irish, which I thought would impress the Irish bartenders in Boston. I made up my parents' names, Timothy and Patty Ryan, and gave Mitch a DOB of April 1, 1930 (April Fools' Day—a wiseass gesture to be sure). I then made up the rest of the demographic and personal information that was required for those old birth certificates, took the falsified document into Boston, and had it reduced and laminated at a photo shop. The photographer on duty figured it was a fake but just smiled about the whole thing—maybe he was Irish. I then had a yeoman friend of mine make me a fake navy ID under the Mitchell Ryan alias and DOB. I used it whenever we went into bars. Even with a perfectly legal-looking navy ID, bartenders would question me—they knew sailors could easily get fake IDs—so I would have to show them the fake birth certificate as well.

"Let's see your ID lad," one bartender said, and I handed him my ID and laminated birth certificate. The bartender stared at them for a while and then said, "Aye, the navy is taken em younger, or I'm getting older." Then he served me, protesting and shaking his head the entire time.

On nights when Rowle—who already looked like he was twenty-one—and I weren't on duty but weren't eligible for liberty, we snuck off the base anyway. Part of the hospital complex was located under the Mystic River Bridge, and the chain-link fence along the waterside was not well maintained or well illuminated. It was filled with holes and other places that were either easy to climb over or crawl through. So Rowle and I would simply "jump the fence" and walk up Broadway to downtown Chelsea. We'd go out and drink at the bars in Chelsea or take the bus to Revere Beach, or we'd go over to Charleston and take the MTA into Boston. We were fearless, careless, and extremely lucky. In fact, the one time we did get into trouble with the shore patrol for being caught out of uniform, we were on an authorized liberty. I always carried my real ID and liberty pass in my jumper pocket and stored the fake stuff in my wallet. This way if I was stopped by the shore patrol or the police, I could easily pull out the real ID without fumbling through my wallet and possibly exposing my fake ID papers.

Illegally drinking and skipping out without a pass weren't the only things Rowle and I did; we also did healthy, teen-age activities and became good friends. As Rowle and I became closer, I found out more about him—where he came from, what his interests were, and why he was in the navy. He had grown up in a small town in Maine that was predominately, to hear him tell it, French speaking and Catholic. They spoke Canadian-style French, so their accent was different from that of a person from Paris. Rowle had graduated from high school and entered the seminary to become a priest because that's what his family wanted, but he dropped out after less than a year and joined the navy—he said it seemed like a good idea at the time. I asked him once, "So why did you drop out of the seminary—'cause of all the bullshit you had to put up with?"

"Very simple, Mike, my friend," he said, "Pussy." Although that didn't shock me, it did surprise me a little because I never really understood the bit about priests never being able to get married. Rowle went on. "I couldn't stand the thought of going through life without fucking. You know priests can't get married and that means no fucking. So I left the seminary without ever telling my family the real reason, I just told them I wanted to have 'other experiences' first and because of the war I wanted to join the navy." What surprised me now was that Rowle went willingly to a seminary first before discovering his need for sex. I didn't think growing up worked that way. I thought Rowle was a street kid, like me, not someone who would want to go to a seminary. I knew guys who went on to Jewish seminaries to become rabbis, but they started out at five or six years old, stayed in Hebrew school after their bar mitzvah, then went on to the various yeshivas or other rabbinical institutions and became rabbis. But that wasn't me, even though my grandfather wanted me to be a rabbi. I generally didn't run around with guys who became rabbis, so Rowle was a new experience for me—a seminarian who could comfortably run on the streets of Chelsea.

*   *   *   *

Chelsea, Massachusetts, was a tough town of working-class Irish, some Jewish entrepreneurs, and a number of gypsies living in converted stores. We ran with a group of former Chelsea High girls who stole Chelsea High jackets for us so that the local teen-age gangs wouldn't beat us up. The young adults in Chelsea didn't like anyone from outside their neighborhood—especially sailors—coming in and mixing with their women. We would go roller-skating at Revere Beach and do all the things that eighteen- and nineteen-year-olds that didn't go to college do. It was from these girls that I got my Boston—actually my Chelsea—accent. It happened in a perfectly normal fashion; I realized I was talking like a native when the girls and old Lieutenant Tibbits no longer sounded funny to me. Being comfortable in this new culture—talking like the locals—made me really feel at home in Chelsea. So, Rowle and I spent many days and evenings just talking, sightseeing, and going into town either on authorized liberty or by going, as the term implied, *over the fence.*

One warm, summer Saturday morning when we were both on liberty, Rowle borrowed a car and asked me to go with him on a short trip. "Where we going— out of town to find some strange pussy?" I asked in a playful manner.

With a silly grin on his face, Rowle shook his head. "Nope, we're going up to Lowell to visit a relative of mine."

Lowell was about a one-hour ride from the hospital. I didn't ask him before we left Chelsea who the relative was or why we were going to Lowell. But as we got on to the highway, and just to start a conversation I asked, "So who is it in Lowell that we're going to see? A cute cousin and her even cuter friend, I hope." I really didn't care why we were going, or who we would see and my voice reflected that; it was just nice to be going out with a friend on a nice weekend day and not be working on the wards of a military hospital.

"No, my horny friend, we're going to visit my sister," he said. "She's living there now. She's a year older than me and she's teaching in a private school in Lowell." So Rowle's sister is a teacher—that's interesting, I thought. Rowle still had that silly grin on his mischievous face, so I knew that something was out of the ordinary.

* * * *

On the trip up to Lowell, I started thinking about my family roots and my cousins. Although I was an only child, my parents came from larger families and always appeared happy about that, even though the larger size often brought financial and emotional hardship. I recall my father talking about how his family came over from Russia in 1908. His parents, Tzvi and Malkah Rabinovich, were in their mid-thirties when they gathered up their four children and prepared them for the long journey to America. Only two years old at the time, my father has no memories of either the trip to America or his home in Russia, but his parents and older siblings told him the story many times. His name was Zelig back then. His siblings' names then were Yankel, the oldest brother at seven; Mikhail, the second youngest brother at four; and Fayge, their sister who was the oldest child at eleven.

My grandfather told them about going across the ocean to a new world. "Children," my Zadie Tzvi said in Yiddish, "we have to leave here because the country is at war and the goyim are making us leave. It will be a long trip, so you have to behave and do what you're told, and then soon we will be with Uncle Chiam in America." My grandmother's brother had left for America from another Russian shtetl over four years ago and had settled with his family in Detroit, Michigan. About two weeks after leaving their village in Russia, the family arrived on the SS *Kherson* at Ellis Island. They entered the country with the stipulation that they would be living with my bubbie's brother Chiam Katz, in Detroit, Michigan. At

Ellis Island, a Jewish agency helped them book train passage to Detroit and sent a telegram to Uncle Chiam saying when he should meet them at the train station.

Uncle Chiam met them with his horse-drawn cart and loaded their few belongings—some clothes, my Zadie Tzvi's tallis and tzvillin, a few pictures, and a little jewelry that Bubbie Malkah was able to smuggle out of Russia. "So, *nu*, how do you like America?" Uncle Chiam asked them in Yiddish.

Aunt Fayge told me how the older children were impressed by the buildings all around the train station and the busy traffic of horse carts, trolleys, and even a few automobiles. "It was a gray winter day," she said, "and there was dirty snow and slush along the street, on the sidewalks, and by the houses. The sidewalks were covered with coal ashes to help people walk without slipping, and the smell of burning coal was strong in the air." The mile-long ride took around fifteen minutes, but even in the cold the kids, all bundled up in old coats and blankets, were thrilled; the older ones remembered it always.

Once at Chiam's house, on Winder Street near Hastings, the family got organized and at Chiam's bidding, immediately Americanized the children. First they changed the family's name to Rabin. Surprisingly, Zadie Tzvi didn't object to this since he had heard that many Jews had changed their names from Rabinovich or Rabinowitz to Rabin; the word still meant "son of a rabbi." My grandfather still wanted to be called Tzvi, but my Grandmother Malkah became Mollie to everyone except her husband. Bubbie Mollie liked the American name, but to Zadie Tzvi she would always be "the Queen" Malkah. Fayge became Faye, which was not much of a change, and Yankel became Jack. Mikhail easily became Michael, but he was always called Mikie (pronounced "MY-key"). Lastly my father, the baby Zelig, became known as Sidney. Neighbors and other relatives helped with the names and said it would be easier for the children in school if they had Americanized names, but in Hebrew school, the boys were still called by their given Yiddish names.

They were in Uncle Chiam's house less than a week when Bubbie Mollie, with the help of a neighbor who spoke broken but understandable English, took all the kids, including my father who was dressed to look older, to the Bishop school. She wanted them enrolled as soon as possible, but they couldn't get in until the fall of 1908—six months later. Being Jews, exact birth dates were hard to come by because Jews never recorded births, only deaths. When the ship's manifest was being written and required ages for the children, Bubbie Mollie made sure that Mikie was listed as five and not his true age of four. She tried to pass my father off as Mikie's twin brother by saying that he was sickly when he was a baby, and that the ship's manifest was wrong. The school secretary didn't fall for it because she knew that Jews believed strongly in early education and would try to get their kids into school before the age of five.

By the end of the summer of 1908, the older children could speak passable English from playing with the neighborhood kids. In the fall Mikie went to kindergarten, and Jack and Faye were placed in second and third grades. However, within a semester Faye was placed in fifth grade and soon went on to her proper grade level in junior high school. Dad started school two years later when he was almost five, but only Mikie was there to guide and protect him—Uncle Jack had only two years left in elementary school and Aunt Faye, in the eighth grade, was already thinking about high school.

* * * *

I stopped daydreaming when we got to Lowell. Rowle drove us to a clean, well kept working-class neighborhood where he pulled up in front of a yellow-brick, institutional-looking building. I didn't have time to read the sign in the front that said something about the building being a parochial school and mentioning the Sisters of St. Denis. As we walked inside, I felt a little uncomfortable to say the least; I had never been in a Catholic church or a school building that looked less like a school than it did some kind of religious sanctuary. The entrance area looked like a church with high ceilings and ornamental walls with various religious pictures neatly hung around and a huge cross with a figure of Christ nailed on it, located right in the most conspicuous part of the wall. We approached the desk in the foyer and Rowle, in his best Frenchville French, told the nun that we were there to visit his sister, Sister Marie Therese. The nun looked at us and replied, "Oui, yes, sister was expecting you and she's waiting for you in the visitor's area down the hall."

I had no idea that Rowle's sister was a nun; in fact, I had no idea he even had a sister until that morning. As it turned out, Rowle had three sisters and two brothers—most of them nuns and priests! Rowle was the second youngest, although they were all only about a year apart in age, as one might expect from a devout Catholic family.

We entered the visitor's area, and after greeting his sister in French and kissing her tenderly on the cheek, Rowle introduced me. Sister Marie was a petite, delicate-looking woman with a pretty face, completely unlike my mental picture of a nun. My image of a nun at that time was more along the lines of a 'female' rabbi—a glowering, unpleasant-looking disciplinarian who would crack you across the knuckles as soon as look at you. Her family resemblance to Rowle—

the long narrow face and slight frame—was certainly there. They exchanged pleasantries in French briefly until Sister Marie pointed out, "Rowle, don't you think that it's a little rude talking in French since your friend Mike doesn't speak French?" So they switched to English. General conversations about the family followed—how were the folks, what were the other brothers and sisters up to, and so on.

Rowle was more interested in knowing about his sister's daily activities. She had started at the school after Rowle went into the navy, and he had been there only one time before, and then only briefly. Rowle asked her, "When I was last here you had just moved in and hadn't settled in. You were a little anxious about what assignments you might get being the new girl on the block; so what are you doing?"

"I'm teaching a class of third-graders—girls, of course, and I really love it!" she said, and she certainly looked like she did. She asked about me—where I was from and the like—and appeared to be truly interested.

"I'm from Detroit, uh ... and I was an art student in high school," I answered awkwardly. I didn't tell her I was Jewish—I'm not sure why, but it didn't seem to be necessary for her to know. After a bit more chit-chat she asked if we would like to see the small chapel in the school. Rowle, of course, said yes. As we were leaving the visitor's area, he whispered, "Just do as I do." We went down the corridor and entered the chapel. When Rowle genuflected and made the sign of the cross, I clumsily did the same and thought for sure that I would be struck dead by lightening, either by my god or theirs for pretending to be a Catholic. There was no one else in the chapel at that time, so we quietly and reverently walked around admiring the old finely hand carved red-oak pews. The sun was streaming through the small stained glass windows onto the altar creating a cacophony of red, green and orange on the floor and the altar that somehow made the colors look like they belonged together. We all commented on how beautiful and spiritual it looked. After a few quiet minutes we went back to the visitor's area to talk some more.

Once back in the visitor's area, Rowle asked his sister, "So, what do you girls do for fun around here?" The way he asked showed sincere concern for her happiness.

Sister Marie started to tell him about some of the other sisters and what they did together. "Oh, we have a great volley ball team, and I'm still a pretty good first-baseman for our baseball team ..."

Rowle interrupted her saying, "No, no ... I mean, do you go out dancing and get drunk once in a while?" Rowle asked. She immediately started to blush and smiled at his good-natured kidding. Then Rowle said, "Look, it's Saturday. How about you finding another good-looking chick for me and then the four of us will go out dancing. What do you think, Mike?"

I was speechless—you weren't supposed to talk to nuns like that, even if they were family. Sister Marie laughed lightly, for she apparently knew her little brother well. She said something in French that sounded to my untrained ears like "Tze a fou!" Rowle told me later that what she had said to him was "You're crazy." There was more giggling and light hearted banter between brother and sister, and the subject was quickly changed back to more acceptable dialogue. "When are you going home to visit?" she asked, and Rowle told her he was planning a trip later this summer. She said, "Well be sure to give my love to everyone and tell them I'm well and they should write."

We left the convent shortly after that and headed back to Chelsea. I was quiet for most of the trip, but I couldn't stop thinking about Rowle's sister and how human she seemed. I thought nuns were like teachers and rabbis in that they weren't quite like the rest of us. They didn't buy things—that's why you were so shocked to see them in stores like everyone else. They never went to movies or watched TV or even listened to the radio. They lived in places we never saw and had rooms full of books where they just sat and read all the time. To actually meet a real nun and talk with her, and then be there while her kid brother joked with her about going on a date with me, was an amazing adventure. I would never forget that Saturday afternoon. The experience would influence me later when, as a corpsman on a ship, I was asked to teach the catechism to another shipmate so that he could convert to Catholicism. I also realized after that day that teachers and rabbis, and other authority figures, were just people you could interact with, without being uncomfortable. They could even have a sense of humor and blush and laugh just like the rest of us—something I had never realized before.

* * * *

Rowle and I made HN during that summer of 1951, and in September, I used my first thirty-day leave from the navy to go home and reacquaint myself with my friends and family. The train for Detroit left around nine in the morning and was scheduled to arrive at the Michigan Central terminal around nine at night—a twelve-hour ride. When I got on the train, the coach car was about half full and I spotted a very cute, thin, dark-haired girl about halfway down the car on the left side of the train. She looked to be around eighteen and was sitting alone next to the window. I was walking from the front to the rear of the train, so I could see the faces of the passengers, and I saw her smile as I moved toward her. That was all the encouragement I needed.

"Anyone sitting here?" I asked. She shook her head without saying anything, but she still had that cute smile on her face. I got my ditty bag settled away—I had plenty of clothes at home, so I had packed only my toiletries and some underwear—and sat down next to her. She then edged closer to me, still wearing that enchanting smile, and acted like she wanted me to talk. She seemed just delighted to be sitting there with me in the seat next to her. Maybe it was my sailor suit, or maybe it was me, or maybe it was both of those things and the fact that we were just two teenagers on a long train ride together, but that's how I met Rose Domokos.

"What's your name, and where are you from?" I asked.

"Rose Domokos, but call me Rosie, and I'm from Detroit," she said with that warm smile, and in a lovely mid-western accent that immediately made me feel right at home. "I just finished school this year—graduated from Immaculata High School in June. Have you heard of it? It's pretty new." Before I could answer, she added, "I just spent six weeks in Boston visiting my aunt and meeting my cousin's friends and having all kinds of fun with them."

Then she looked at me like she was waiting for me to tell her what I was about. So I told her. "My name's Mike Rabin—I'm also from Detroit, and, yeah, I know where Immaculata is—I graduated from Cass Tech last year." This was a lie, of course, since I really just quit school, but I wanted to impress her. I was afraid that if I told her I was a dropout, she would no longer want to talk with me. "I'm stationed at Chelsea Naval Hospital," I continued. "What kind of a name is Domokos?"

In the 1950s, it wasn't unusual or rude for people to ask such personal questions. I thought that she would say Greek, but she said Hungarian. Detroit had many ethnic neighborhoods, and I was trying to place the Hungarian section of town when she said that she lived on the southwest side, near Livernois and Michigan Avenue. I said, "Isn't Immaculata far from that part of town; I thought all the brainy girls went there?" We talked a little more about school, and the type of music we liked. "I like to listen to modern jazz like Stan Kenton." I paused briefly then said, "I really missed hearing "Beautiful Carl in Boston." Carl was the local DJ who played hip music like jazz "is he still on the air in Detroit?" I was talking fast with that typical teen-age excitability in my voice. "What do you listen to?" I asked.

She answered with a little distaste in her voice, "I don't like that modern jazz stuff; I like hillbilly and cowboy music, and who's Beautiful Carl?" She waited briefly, and then continued, "No, not every girl that goes to Immaculata is a brain."

Well, nobody's perfect I thought, but I didn't say it. We continued from school and music to movies to sports—we were both Tiger fans. I told her, "Yeah, I love the Tigers; some of my cousins went to the World Series in '45. They sat in the bleachers but it was great. I use to usher some of the games with my cousin."

She seemed really interested and told me, "You know I live almost within walking distance from Briggs Stadium. My brother use to usher there too; did you know him? His name is Ralph, Ralph Domokos. He took me to a bunch of games; I saw Greenberg and Newhouser play." Her eyes glowed when she talked about the Tigers and our conversation became more and more relaxed as we began to know each other and start to like each other.

* * * *

After a few hours of getting to know each other, the hormones of two teenage kids—essentially alone on a train—began to kick in. We started slowly at first, like when you meet someone in the movie theater on a Saturday afternoon. In the late 1940s, teenage boys would go the movies on Saturday afternoons and look for girls sitting in pairs without any other boys around. We would sit next to them and start conversations, and soon we would be "necking." So, it was quite natural for me to put my arm around Rosie's shoulder while we continued to make small talk. I had broken up earlier in the summer with my girl friend in Detroit, so it was nice to find someone else from home that I could be with. Soon, just like in the movie theater, the kissing started and then some furtive petting under her sweater. We were careful not to draw attention to ourselves, and the seats in coach were high enough that unless someone was sitting across from us or walking by, they really couldn't see what we were doing. The talking and petting was just getting heavy when we broke for lunch. I treated her to a ham sandwich and a small bottle of chocolate milk—how non-kosher can you get!—which I bought from a stall by the tracks at one of the train stops. We ate little else the rest of that day. I really felt comfortable and liked being with her, and she apparently liked being with me.

By late afternoon our talking and making out had become more intense, and we began to attract the attention of some of the older passengers who were making it their business to walk by and stare at us with rather derisive looks. We really didn't care and thought it was cute to upset some of the old folks on the train, but the passion was rising and about seven in the evening, after almost a whole day of sexual foreplay, we decided to do something about our privacy. I told her to go to the head—the lavatory—at the front of the car and that I would follow her in about five minutes. She went straight down the aisle, into the head, and closed the door. Well, I didn't wait five minutes, but followed almost right after her. As I looked back before going in, I could tell that some of the travelers knew what was going on by their shocked expressions.

When I first came into the head we were so worked up and so titillated by the apparent illicitness of what we were doing that we couldn't stop giggling. After a full day of sex play, and the added excitement of being in the train's head together, we were both very amenable to having sex—but it wasn't meant to be. The restrooms on trains in those days were tiny: a little sink with foot pedals for the water faucet and a toilet that flushed right on to the tracks were about it. I no sooner got in and bolted the door, when we both realized that the space was much too small to do anything in a horizontal position. We stood close together with her back against the door and continued to do a little more necking, or as it was called in those days, dry humping. But it soon became apparent that the small, unseemly, cramped space had turned both of us off. Without saying a word, we stopped. I washed my hands and face, straightened my uniform, combed my hair, and then left to allow her to straighten her clothes in private.

After the disappointment of not being able to get more intimate anywhere on the train, I went back to our seats and imagined the scene the way I had wanted it to be. I pictured Rosie's skirt up to her neck and her little white cotton panties down around one of her legs. I pictured her being so wet that it would just be a matter of seconds before I would be inside her, and only a few seconds more that both of us would explode. I pictured both of us having orgasms one after the other, all with her in a standing position, one of her legs resting on the sink, the other on the ground, my hands grasping her firm, little butt and her arms around me. How spectacular it would have been. I also imagined seeing her tits. I had felt them under her sweater and blouse but not under her bra. They were small but firm and felt so marvelous. I pictured us having the time to take off her sweater and blouse and bra, and getting the chance to see and touch her naked breasts. Oh, my god! I was getting all worked up again.

When Rosie came back to our seats, she had that cute little smile on her face, her skirt all neat and her sweater unruffled. Her white bobby socks still looked spotless, and her blue and white saddle oxfords were not at all scuffed. She smelled of institutional soap, or whatever sort of soap they had on trains, and I really enjoyed looking at her and tasting her natural, young-woman sweetness. When she sat down, she immediately closed her eyes and cuddled up to me. We both rested for about an hour or so before the train came into Detroit. There would be no more sex play that day.

While I was holding her, I began to feel sad—or maybe I was feeling guilty. I knew that I would probably never see her again, as likeable as I found her. I wasn't sure that what we almost did in the restroom was somehow all right, but I was now relieved that we didn't have sex—even though I knew that this was post World War II and sexual morality had changed. Young people could now engage in sex without guilt or lifelong commitment. This was true especially in wartime, and 1951 was wartime. But as I thought about what might have happened if she had become pregnant, I felt guilty anyway. Maybe she had thought that we had something going and I would be obligated to see her again. Maybe I would even have to take care of her—just like in the movies. I knew I hadn't tried to coerce her into sex—she was just as aggressive as I was, maybe even more so—so it wasn't that. Then again, maybe I was just beginning to grow up, and now that my youthful fantasies were becoming real possibilities, reality had set in.

After once hearing me talking about picking up girls at Revere Beach, Major Grady Dumont had told me, "Remember, Mike, your wildest dreams can turn out to be your worst nightmares." I think maybe I was just a little scared that this could have turned out to be one of those nightmares.

As we pulled into the station in Detroit, we exchanged telephone numbers and addresses; she told me, "Mike honey, my family is going to be at the station; do you mind if maybe we don't get off the train together? You being a sailor and all, they may not understand, okay?"

I could understand that she didn't want her family to know that she had gotten friendly with a sailor on the train, so I said, "Hey, sweetie not a problem. When I get home and get back into my civvies I'll call you in a day or two and then I can come over and meet them." I got off the train first and saw my dad in the large entry area of the station, watching the crowd, looking for me to come out of the track area. I went up and gave him a hug and a kiss, and he returned my warm greeting. I noticed Rosie pass by without looking at me, searching for her family. I nodded in her direction to my father and said, "See that girl over there in the plaid skirt and sweater?" He nodded and I said, or rather, lied, "I screwed her every way possible on the train ride home." He looked surprised and didn't indicate approval or disapproval—just mild curiosity. I thought he would be proud of me now that I had grown up; but just maybe he was thinking that his son hadn't grown up as much as I thought I did.

✳   ✳   ✳   ✳

I spent my leave visiting old haunts with my friends, enjoying the freedom of being able to go out whenever I wanted to without having to get permission. I never did contact Rosie while on leave, but I thought of her often. I also never discussed her again with my father, and he never asked about her even after we got home from the train station. My father did, however, ask me, "Why are you talking so funny? You never talked like that before."

"Funny you should say that to me because I was thinking how you sound funny!" We both got a laugh out of that exchange and in a short time Dad sounded fine and I guess I did too. At that point in my young life, talking with a Chelsea accent was as natural to me as putting on my navy uniform with all its thirteen buttons and flaps. Putting on my uniform seemed strange at first, but in a very short time I couldn't remember when I didn't button my pants that way or when my Chelsea friends sounded strange. When my leave was over, I took the train back to Boston but didn't meet anyone interesting or fun; the twelve-hour trip was boring and anticlimactic.

In retrospect, I found that two of the most influential women in my life up to that time were a nun who erased my misconceptions about people of authority and a girl on a train who made me realize that sex can be far more complicated than I originally thought. But I was pleased about all of this, for it made the future far more exciting and offered the promise of a young adulthood filled with other interesting women. Some of these women would nurture me emotionally and some would nurture me spiritually. Sister Marie and Rosie did both—how wonderful was that?

✳   ✳   ✳   ✳

During the time I was at Chelsea, I served on SOQ and on the isolation, or contagious diseases, wards. Once I made HN, I started to volunteer for the marines every time a request for volunteers was posted. The navy preferred to take volunteers who had a full year of hospital service and were about to be promoted to HM3, but if they needed a lot of volunteers, they would then take the senior HNs. In either case, I was never selected. After my six months on the wards, I was able to get an assignment in the urology department as a genitourinary (GU) tech. I learned to do a variety of tasks, including a number of X-ray diagnostic procedures, and I assisted the doctors with various urological procedures.

I continued to volunteer for the marines, but as my time for promotion to HM3 neared, I began to consider other options—in case I would actually have an option. Independent sea duty looked appealing because very few officers and senior servicemen would be around to tell you what to do. I thought that would be really neat to be able to treat guys on my own, especially if I was able to go into combat. Then by some lucky break—perhaps my name was in the right place at the right time—I did get an independent duty assignment aboard a destroyer. It was an Atlantic fleet destroyer—not the Pacific, where the war was—but I was okay with that. I would go to my new assignment and do my job as best I could, and if the opportunity to go into battle came, I would be thankful for the chance. However, I no longer felt that I had to go into combat to become a man. And little did I know that the people I would soon be meeting aboard ship would be a whole new adventure in itself. I also didn't know that independent sea duty would require me to assume more responsibility than I thought I would ever have to manage.

Chapter 4

1952—BOBBY JOHNSON

Bobby Johnson was an overweight, not very sharp seaman first who was in serious need of becoming my striker. A striker is someone who wants to earn a rating that either requires schooling or some specialized skills. In order to get that rating, he has to "strike" for it in a way similar to a civilian apprenticeship. If the striker became proficient enough to convince the navy that he could do the job by testing for a petty officer rank, then he could get the rating. Most seamen apprentices are recent boot camp graduates who go on to become boatswain's mates, gunner's mates, or some other shipboard rating. Not Bobby Johnson; he really wanted to be a corpsman—a "pecker checker." Rarely do you find corpsman strikers aboard ship, but here was Seaman Johnson just waiting for me to come onboard. He was sure that if he could be my striker, then somehow the navy would send him to corps school and he would become a regular navy corpsman. When he took his navy placement tests in boot camp, he told me, "I'm a poor fuckin' student, never could study or do shit like that so I didn't score high enough on the fuckin' intelligent tests, or whatever the fuck they were, to get into school. I just went to sea after boot camp, but I know I can be a good fuckin' corpsman." Not getting into corps school didn't stop Bobby Johnson from trying. A personnelman in boot camp told him that his scores at that time were too low to attend any naval school and that he should try to get assigned as a corpsman striker for a while—

six months or a year. Then if the commanding officer recommended him, he might be able to get into corps school. When I met Bobby, he had close to three years in the navy, on land and sea, and although he tried, no one ever let him work as a corpsman striker at any of his other duty stations.

I had been temporarily stationed in Boston at First Naval District Headquarters for a couple of weeks in March of 1952. I was waiting to start my new assignment of independent duty on a destroyer. The ship was due to return from a shakedown cruise after refitting, and I was delighted when I got word that it would be arriving the next day. I was told to be ready to board her at the Charleston Naval Ship Yard. From that first drizzly day that I came onboard the USS *Bock*, DDE 483, in early April of 1952, Bobby was on my case to be my striker. The *Bock* was more or less a modern, refitted destroyer escort with a crew of around 225—somewhat smaller than a regular full sized destroyer. I think that because the *Bock* was much smaller than the other ships Bobby served on, he felt his chances of becoming a striker were much better. He saw me coming along the gangplank, and almost before I could request permission to come onboard from the officer of the deck, Bobby was there to greet me with a big, dumb smile on his round, pink face. "Hey Doc, I'm Johnson, seaman first, and I got permission to be your striker." I had no idea what he was talking about—exactly who had given him permission to be my striker?

I just had my new HM3 rating sewn on my jumper, so I was a little surprised that some SN would be so deferential to me; I was the lowest-ranking petty officer, actually just one step up from Johnson in rank. He seemed harmless enough, and escorted me below to the small quarters where all seventeen of the ship's service personnel were bunked—carrying my seabag, I might add. After Bobby told me about not getting into corps school after boot camp, he told me, "You know it's important that you have a striker. You're a fuckin' third class petty officer now, and you need a striker to paint sick bay when it needs a fresh coat—about every six months. I'll also keep sick bay swabbed and clean, and I'll be around to help you out when I'm needed. Shit, you can't ask for more."

"And what do I have to do for you?" I asked. "It seems I get a deck ape for free to do all the shit details. What's in it for you?"

Bobby said, "All you gotta do is to teach me enough so that I can get a fuckin' recommendation from the CO for going to corps school; that's all you gotta do." Bobby tried to act like being my striker was a done deal, but it was obvious that I had to approve his transfer as a deck hand before he could actually get the assignment.

I was supposed to report to a chief petty officer (CPO) corpsman onboard, and I figured it should be his responsibility to pick our striker, as there would be the two of us working in sick bay. I told Johnson, "Hey, let me get settled in and when I meet with the chief, I'll talk with him about you being our striker, okay? And by the way, do you know of any other seamen onboard who might want to be corpsman strikers?"

That made Bobby a little nervous, and he said, "Look, I know that I'm the only fucker on this pig iron hunk of shit that wants to be your fuckin' striker—I'm absolutely sure of that!" He said it like he had taken some kind of survey. He offered to take me to meet Chief Hospital Corpsman Oldendorf, but I told him that I could do that myself and that I would be in touch later. Not wanting to make a pest of himself, he took the hint and left quickly.

Down in the service personnel quarters—where cooks, bakers, the laundryman, the yeoman and even me, the corpsman—are bunked I met a few of the other ship's service personnel. We introduced ourselves and they showed which bunk and locker were mine; I stowed my gear and got settled in. They appeared pleased to see me come aboard—I guess they appreciated the need for the ship's corpsman.

*   *   *   *

The crew, in general, treat corpsmen on independent duty with some regard because they never know when they might need medical assistance. If they ever do need a corpsman's service, they want to be sure that the corpsman has nothing against them. The HM3 I replaced was there to show me sick bay and tell me my duties. He knew when I was coming onboard today and was packed and ready to leave for his next duty station before I even arrived. Sick bay is a small space about ten feet by ten feet square. There was a high desk, a table and chair, storage cabinets and an emergency operating table that folded up on the aft bulkhead. The working space over the storage cabinets had a microscope secured to it and some rudimentary laboratory equipment. My predecessor showed me around sick bay, which took all of five minutes, and gave me the door key and his brown, navy-issue jackknife. I examined the gnarly handle and the two blades—one of which was very sharp—wondering why I needed a jackknife or what I would use it for. With a quick handshake and a nod, the former ship's corpsman took off for his next tour of duty. I hung around sick bay a little longer to look over the library: *Gray's Anatomy*, *The Merck Manual*, the *U.S. Pharmacopeia*, and *New and Nonofficial Remedies*. I put my *Handbook of the Hospital Corps* on the library shelf, familiarized myself with the locations of various medical supplies, and went looking for the chief.

CPO Oldendorf was in his bunk; he looked very casual with his jacket off, shirt unbuttoned, and no tie. He was a short, balding, heavyset man in his early to mid-thirties who was regular navy and would be eligible for retirement in about another eight years. After introducing myself, I asked him about his military history.

"I was a corpsman stationed with the navy liaison office at Tripler Army Hospital in Hawaii when the war broke out," he said in clipped sentences. "I got promoted to chief because of the speeded up wartime promotion process, but I'm not really keen on the medical side of being a corpsman. I was essentially a bookkeeper, and that's all I really expect to do. You'll have the responsibility of being the medical corpsman attending to sick call and treating anyone injured onboard, okay?" I nodded in agreement and felt good about the fact that I wouldn't just be his medical assistant, but I would be doing the treating. I felt that my experience at Chelsea Hospital and my schooling, as brief as it was, were enough for me to be able to handle the job.

The chief continued. "I'll handle the books—ordering supplies, keeping the crew's medical records, and the like."

Oldendorf seemed easy enough to get along with and our separate duties seemed well defined. I asked the chief, "Do you think I need a striker for helping me keep up sick bay?"

He immediately smiled and started shaking his head from side to side. "You mean Chubby Johnson?"

I was smiling too, and I told the chief that Bobby Johnson had already approached me. "Bobby said he wanted to be our striker, but I told him that I would have to check with you first," I said.

Oldendorf continued to shake his head as he told me that Johnson was somewhat of a pain in the ass and a joke to the rest of the crew; the previous corpsman hadn't wanted a striker, but most of all, he hadn't wanted Johnson. "Johnson keeps telling everyone how one day he'll go to corps school and become a regular navy hospital corpsman," Oldendorf said. "Right now Johnson's just a deck-ape, and most of his fellow crewmen think that he'll probably retire as a deck ape after thirty years in the navy."

I guess that didn't surprise me; I could easily see how they could feel that way about Bobby, but he didn't strike me as being a total pain in the ass, and he seemed to know when to back off.

Then Oldendorf went on to say, "Bobby wouldn't be a problem; the crew generally liked him and if you want a striker to do errands and field-day tasks, I couldn't care less who you pick." After a little more general conversation, the chief told me that he would meet me in sick bay the next morning at 0830 for sick call.

When I walked into sick bay the next morning, Bobby Johnson was already there and so was the chief. By the big grin on Bobby's round, almost cherubic, face, I assumed that Oldendorf might have already told Bobby that he could be my striker. A few sailors were waiting for sick call, but it was nothing serious; in fact, most were there just to see me, the new corpsman, and get to know what I was about. After I was talking with the other crew members for a while, the chief asked, "So, Mike, do you want Johnson as your striker?"

I guess the chief hadn't told him but I felt that I couldn't refuse without really insulting the guy, and to some extent, I was relieved to have someone who knew about shipboard life and was apparently easy to get along with. "Sure, he'll be fine," I said, and Bobby heaved a big sigh of relief. Everyone was all smiles to see that Johnson was finally going to be a corpsman striker. Seeing that I had control of things, Oldendorf said that if I needed him he would be in the chief's quarters. For the rest of the morning, Bobby acted like an older big brother, ready to take care of me no matter what. He introduced me to everyone who came by with little stories about who each person was. Many greeted him as Chubby, but I decided to call him Bobby, which is what he preferred.

One of the crew he introduced me to was a deck ape named Jim Zeck. With some derision, Bobby told me that Zeck was originally an Ohio farmer and had been in the navy for a long time. Zeck made an impression because of the way he looked at me. He didn't say much, and he didn't have any ailment to complain about. It seems that he was there just to see if Bobby would be my striker. He had a dirty face and beady, mean-looking eyes, and he was carrying a small length of hemp line like it was his job to do something with it. Bobby confirmed what my instincts were telling me about Zeck: he was a mean son of a bitch, a troublemaker who was always looking to start a fight. I knew I should avoid him, but I felt in my bones from the way he stared at me with something akin to a sneer on his face that Zeck and I would someday cross paths in a very unpleasant manner.

* * * *

Corpsmen and other service-rated personnel, like cooks, storekeepers, and laundrymen, were in what were called "cumshaw" (pronounced "COM-shaw") positions. That meant that we were able to give out goods and services for which we, in turn, would get other goodies. For instance, I could write a chit for somebody to get some blood work done on the base, or the tender, and give him a return time of late afternoon. He would never go for the blood work, of course, but the chit itself was like a base liberty pass. If I did this for the yeoman, he would make me a fake ID; the cooks would make lemonade, and I would add ethyl alcohol so that we could drink mock Tom Collins's aboard the ship. It was the cumshaw element of being a corpsman that Bobby liked most.

He loved the power that went with being able to ask me for lab chits, or other such things, to give to his buddies. He never overdid it, and I always made sure he didn't abuse it. I never asked him what favors he got in return, but he knew that money or any items of real value were not allowed. But somehow he always had lots of help when we needed sick bay painted or really scrubbed down.

Bobby also had a sincere interest in practicing first aid and learning other corpsmen skills—sewing up a wound, bandaging injuries, and dispensing medicines such as cough syrup and vitamins. I wouldn't let him do anything medical, not even give out cough medicine, unless I was there. Bobby knew that until he graduated from corps school, he wouldn't be allowed to do most of the medical procedures on his own, he just wanted to learn them.

To teach him general first aid, I once took a piece of flat rubber about three inches square and almost a sixteenth of an inch thick, cut a slit through it about two inches long, and taught him how to sew up a wound using a simple, curved suture needle and two Alice clamps. I showed Bobby the technique for sewing up the wound, stitch by stitch, spacing the sutures about a half inch apart and tying each one off with a square knot using only the Alice clamps. He practiced every day for about a month until he had it down, and even after that I would often find him practicing on that piece of rubber, putting in four or five stitches at just the right intervals.

He would also try to read the few medical books we had, even though he wasn't always able to accurately read or understand most of the terms. He would ask me how to pronounce the words and to explain what the terms meant in words he could understand.

I remember the time he found the chemical compound "Sodiumdiaminodihydroxyarsenobenzenemethanolsulfoxylate" listed in the *Handbook of the Hospital Corps*. Salvarsan, a trade name, was the more common term for the medicine. At fifty-four letters, the chemical compound was the longest single word (actually, compound word) in the handbook. Bobby couldn't wait to show it to me and ask all about it. Little did he know that most corpsmen knew about the drug's long name. When I was in corps school, I had bet a fellow corpsman that I could pronounce and spell it in less than ten minutes (I won the bet). So, when Bobby asked, "What the fuck is this all about? Are there lots of words like this that I have to know?" What the fuck is goin on here?"

While Bobby was asking me this I took out a piece of paper and without even looking at the book, wrote it out. "You mean this?" I said callously. Needless to say, poor Bobby was not only awed, he was outright depressed because he thought that he might have to memorize the spelling when he went to school—something he thought he could never do. When I saw the hurt and disappointment in his eyes, I realized just how cruel it was for me to have done that. He quickly closed the book and put it back on the shelf.

Later I explained to Bobby, "That long term for Salvarsan is just a bunch of chemical terms. Medicines like that are sometimes described by their chemical contents, but most of the time they just use short names. No one would expect you to memorize terms like that; I had just done it in corps school for a lark and to win a bet from some smart ass guy from the East." Bobby seemed much relieved, and I thought afterward that I would never again put Bobby down or ridicule him when he was truly trying to learn something.

*   *   *   *

Every sailor aboard ship has two duties—his rating and his combat duty. That meant that even the cook and the laundryman had to operate the quad forties (antiaircraft guns), load powder and shells into the five-inch guns, or torpedoes into the torpedo tubes—that is, everyone except corpsmen. The Geneva Convention identifies corpsmen and medics as noncombatants; as a result they are not allowed to load or fire any weapons, at least in theory. So when general quarters (GQ) was sounded telling everyone on board to go to their battle stations, my duty station was the aft emergency operating room located in the aft crew's head. In the head there was a foldaway emergency operating table that came to rest just above the toilet seats. The autoclave was also located in the aft crew's head, along with some cabinets containing sterile supplies for combat casualties. It was part of Bobby's duties to keep the supply cabinets full and to sterilize the emergency operating kits in the autoclave when their sterilization dates had expired. When Bobby became my striker, he decided that he no longer had to report for combat duty, and so he hung around on the fantail with me during GQ; the fantail was located just off of the crew's head. I don't know how he got away with it, but somehow he must have convinced one of the ensigns—we had two onboard—

that as a corpsman striker he was a noncombatant and couldn't man any weapons. Bobby may not have been very smart, but he did know his way around navy rules and regulations.

As a corpsman I had it relatively easy at sea being in a non-combat situation. Most of our ship's time at sea was spent in various fleet exercises and weapons' practice. On many occasions, our ship would run plane guard for the aircraft carriers. Our refitted destroyer specialized in antisubmarine warfare, so our ship's major role was to protect the carriers and larger ships in the fleet from submarine attacks. With the exception of morning sick call and the occasional mass inoculations (immunization shots for overseas visits), I did little else except stay prepared for battle conditions. Unless a medical emergency occurred onboard, such as cuts needing to be sewn up or broken bones set and put in temporary casts, my job was pretty relaxed. I was, however, responsible for VD prevention. I would issue prophylactics, and if sailors returned from shore leave claiming that they had sexual encounters, I would make sure they received prophylaxis kits, or "pros."

In the early 1950s, the navy got rid of the older pro kits and replaced them with a new procedure that simply consisted of a penicillin pill. Then late in 1952, the VD prevention protocol was changed again to include a small cup of hexachlorophene soap along with the penicillin pill. The sailors were instructed to swallow the pill with water and then take the soap and thoroughly wash their genital area at a wash basin or in the shower.

VD training sessions were held on the fantail where we showed old World War II VD prevention movies. I gave lectures before the movies were shown to guarantee that everyone would sit through the talk if they wanted to see the movie. The company was particularly fond of a line of dialogue from one of the movies—"Gee, doc, but she looked so clean"—which they would repeat in unison every time the movie was shown. The final piece of prevention was a written explanation with clear diagrams on how to carry out the new pro procedure; the documents were passed out to the entire crew, including the officers.

The first time the new pro was to be used, Bobby and I prepared a number of cups, each containing one penicillin pill, and a similar number of cups filled with soap. As expected, many of the sailors returned from liberty a little to a whole lot drunk, and they came into sick bay asking for the new pro treatment. I slowly repeated the proper procedure: "Swallow the pill with water, and then take the soap and go wash up in the head or shower."

I then asked, "Now, do you really understand the procedure?" When they said yes, I would nod to Bobby to give each of them two cups—one with the pill, one with soap—and then watch as a number of them put the pill in their mouths and tried to swallow it down with the soap! Of course, those that did swallow any of the soap would immediately get sick and start to upchuck, so we moved our pro station out on deck; if anyone did swallow some soap before we could stop them, we could get them to puke over the side. Bobby was amazed at how stupid these guys were. He just couldn't understand how they could have missed the whole thing after all the publicity and training we had done on the new pro procedure. The saddest part about the military prophylactic process was that many sailors took pros just to make the other guys think they got laid, when in fact, most of them hadn't gotten laid at all. Those who did get laid more than likely made it with a prostitute and usually came back sober and knowing what to do with the pill and soap. It was good for Bobby to see that he wasn't the dumbest kid on the block. In fact, many of his shipmates were apparently dumber than he was which began to give him some sorely needed self-confidence.

*　　*　　*　　*

Bobby had a girlfriend in Norfolk and was planning to get married. According to his old deck-ape buddies, the girl was supposedly a little on the loose side, fairly homely, and just looking for a sailor husband so that she could get a government allotment check. In addition, she was Catholic and insisted that Bobby convert before she would marry him. A number of Bobby's old buddies wanted me to talk him out of marrying her. I met her once briefly, when she and some of her friends put on an "underprivileged kids" party aboard the ship. The women showed up with a bunch of little kids, and the crew entertained them in the mess hall with cake and ice cream, toys, and other presents purchased with our donated funds. As it turned out, the kids were from a Catholic orphanage in the Norfolk area. The women, about six of them—some were sailor's wives—were volunteers at the church and were just trying to make the kids feel a little better about their situation. The kids were over five but under thirteen, so they stood little chance of ever getting adopted and knew it. I never really appreciated the need for family and, as an only child, didn't really think I had any family. In some sense I thought that I could identify with these orphans, but when I thought more about it I realized how wrong I was.

I remember my father telling me about how his parents first survived their lives in the United States. My grandparents, Tzvi and Mollie, moved out of Uncle Chiam's house within the first year of their arrival. Chiam had a fruit-and-vegetable business that he ran out of the Eastern Market year-round with help from his wife and kids. Known as Hyman the Peddler, he also sold fresh vegetables in the summer from his horse-drawn cart that he took around the neighborhood. He didn't like it if anyone called him Hymie, and with a big smile immediately tell them his name is Chiam. He did this because he knew that non-Jews used Hymie as a derogatory term for Jews. Uncle Chiam got Zadie Tzvi a job at a nearby poultry store as a shochet, which is what my zadie did in Russia, along with tending a small farm where he raised chickens for food and bartering. The shochet's job in America paid well enough, and the family got a lot of free chicken parts for soup, schmaltz, and whatever else Bubbie Mollie could do with them; she came up with a great chicken fricassee recipe that the family was still making when I was growing up. The poultry store where Zadie Tzvi worked was on Hastings Street, the heart of the Jewish neighborhood in the early 1900s, and the language of the street was Yiddish, so everyone felt at home there; everyone was family.

By the time my father and his siblings were all enrolled in school, things were fairly good. They had family, friends, and a Russian-Yiddish cultural environment that was warm and protective—almost like the shtetl, but without the fear of Cossacks. Zadie Tzvi joined the Ashkenazi shul and made Uncle Jack come and daven with him during the high holidays. Uncle Mikie didn't go to shul regularly because he was not the davening type, and my father was still too young to sit for long services. The kids never went to school on the major and most of the minor Jewish holidays. Bubbie would cook great holiday dinners even when I was growing up except, of course, on Yom Kippur. Bubbie would also prepare the Pesach Seders which were always at Bubbie and Zadie's house. In fact, the Seders are still held at their house, but now my bubbie has help from my mom and my aunts and older cousins.

During this early period in my family's history, Zadie Tzvi carefully saved his money and by 1920 he was able to open his own kosher poultry store on Dexter Boulevard, near Monterey in the center of the new Jewish section of Detroit. After buying the store, Zadie moved his family to the lower floor of a duplex on Richton Street on Detroit's west side. He joined the B'nai Moshe synagogue on Dexter and Lawrence. And when Uncle Jack was just a year out of high school, Zadie Tzvi made him his partner in the store.

Daily life then was filled with family—from their work, their shul, their language, their culture, and just about everything else they did. Seeing the orphaned kids on the ship made me aware of how much family I really did have. So even though Bobby's girlfriend was significantly overweight, quite homely, and her voice was not the most pleasant-sounding when she spoke or laughed, I did have a warm feeling for what she was trying to do. Even more important, Bobby truly liked her. In fact, it was Bobby who had arranged for the kids' party aboard the ship. He got permission to bring civilians onboard, collected the money, went with his girlfriend and her pals to buy the party supplies and gifts, and arranged transportation—the whole megillah. After seeing how hard he worked to please her (and I suspect himself as well), I had no intention of trying to talk him out of marrying her. Who knows what makes a happy couple, and far be it from me—barely out of my teens—to judge Bobby's personal goals and dreams.

✻ ✻ ✻ ✻

About a week after the kid's party, Bobby came into sick bay with a booklet, maybe ten pages in length, with a short title that had something to do with a convert's catechism. Bobby gave it to me and asked, "Mike, help me learn this shit. I need to pass some kind of a fuckin' test before the fuckin' priest would let me be a holy-fuckin'-Roman-Catholic and marry Carmen." He said with obvious distaste and no doubt some trepidation that he might fail.

I had very little knowledge of Christian religions other than what I had learned from Rowle at Chelsea Naval and what I had seen on our brief trip to visit Sister Marie. At first I was simply going to say no, but I told him, "Bobby, you should find a Catholic sailor onboard who could really teach it to you the right way—I'm not sure I could do it right."

He detected my uneasiness, and knowing that I was Jewish, probably thought that was why I seemed indecisive about teaching him the catechism. In any case, he said in a very conciliatory voice, almost pleading, "Look, Mike, you've been teaching me every fuckin' thing I know about being a corpsman, and you do it without making me feel like a stupid asshole. Now since you taught me every fuckin' thing that's important to me now, it's only right you teach me this shit, too." I recalled how gentle Sister Marie had appeared to me, with her sense of humor and aura of kindness. The fact that she was a teacher, too, also impressed me. I felt that maybe for some reason I owed her this, so I told Bobby that I would help him.

I learned much later that the convert's catechism we were using was a much-abbreviated version of an entire catechism. Like most catechisms, it was arranged in questions and answers, such as:

Q: Who is God?
A: God is the Creator of Heaven and Earth and of all things therein.

Some of the questions dealt with the Ten Commandments. Some dealt with certain un-provable fundamentals of the religion, with answers simply stating that these were, "... mysteries, and we must wait for God to unveil them to us in heaven." In addition, the booklet included instructions on how to perform the rosary: the number of times and the order in which to say the Our Fathers, Hail Marys, and the rest of the ritual. After going through it a few times, I knew it by heart because I could easily memorize this type of material. Our study method was that I would simply ask the questions and Bobby was supposed to give me the right answers. I might also ask him to recite the rosary prayers or maybe the Lord's Prayer. After a couple of weeks of me almost constantly badgering him, Bobby had pretty much mastered it—that is, he could answer all the questions with very few mistakes. What amazed him was that I never needed to look in the book; I simply told him the answer, made him repeat it, and we would go on. He never doubted that I had given him the right answer or that I had fully memorized all the prayers.

Bobby and Carmen, his fiancée, had also been taking other instructions from their priest on living life as a good Catholic, and they had to complete some tasks before Bobby was allowed to take his conversion test. It was actually around a month or so after he started to work on the catechism that they went into Norfolk for their test. Bobby was all dressed up on that day; he wore his clean dress blues, his white hat all bleached and spotless, and his hands and face were freshly scrubbed. He looked just like the little kids I saw in the movies going off to their first communion. I was actually quite proud of him and was a little anxious when he got back. I hoped he hadn't said "fuck" too often in front of the priest. I could tell by his smile and mannerisms that he must have passed which I didn't doubt he would but I knew he had doubts. He couldn't wait to tell me that he was a practicing Catholic now, able to take communion and get married and raise Catholic kids. I congratulated him and wished him much happiness and lots of luck—I must admit that I felt he needed more luck than anything else. Bobby did get married a few months later, and much to the surprise of some of his shipmates, the marriage lasted more than a week. In fact, when I left the ship about eight months later, Bobby was still married—no kids yet, but they were married.

*   *   *   *

My day with Jim Zeck happened at about the same time that Bobby was on leave to get married so he wasn't around to protect me from Zeck. One morning during sick call, a group of about four sailors were waiting around sick bay for cough medicine, APCs, and other minor treatments. Jim Zeck came up to sick bay, pushed everyone out of the way, and demanded some Merthiolate for a scratch on his hand. Everyone backed off because Zeck had that look in his eye like he would kill anyone who would protest. He was obviously agitated—probably because some petty officer had chewed him out—so he used the scratch as an excuse to leave his area.

Everyone was looking at me to see what I would do. "Jim, these guys are ahead of you," I said calmly. "If you wait a couple of minutes, I'll take care of you, okay?"

Zeck angrily sputtered, "Fuck them! I'm bleeding, so you gotta take care of me now!"

I looked at his scratch. "Jim, cool it. It's not even bleeding, and you can easily wait your turn."

With that Zeck spun around and started to walk away, mumbling under his breath. All I could hear was something about "you fuckin' Jews are all alike," and that set me off. As the only Jew aboard ship and the only corpsman, I knew that if I didn't respond I would no longer have the respect of the crew. I knew I was going to get my ass kicked, but I also knew that any fight would be broken up quickly.

I was carrying my navy jackknife, which everyone aboard ship knew I kept sharpened and honed like a razor. I would use it to shave men's arms or legs when they got injured and needed stitches or other such treatment, so it was a given that the knife was to be respected. I pulled out the knife and went screaming after Zeck. "You talk to me like that? I'm gonna cut your fuckin' balls off! I'm gonna cut your dick off and throw it over the side, and then I'm gonna cut your fuckin' throat!" Three of the four guys there grabbed me and held me back before I reached Zeck, although I really didn't struggle much to get away. Zeck was surprised by my suddenly belligerent response; nobody ever challenged him physically like that before and he didn't seem to know how to respond. It seems he was usually the aggressor and started the fights.

The fourth guy in sick bay, the ship's laundryman, was a big fellow and got in front of Zeck, saying, "Hey Jim, you best be going on your way before doc gets loose with that knife o' his. If you kill him you'll be in real deep shit."

After Zeck was gone and things quieted down, I treated the other sailors pretty much in silence. Word passed through the ship that I took on Zeck and didn't get the shit kicked out of me. Zeck and I pretty much ignored each other after that, but I never felt threatened by him again. When Bobby came back from leave and heard about the Zeck incident he seemed quite pleased by it all saying, "So I heard you took on that dumb fuckin' ass Ohio farmer. I told you he was a mean cocksucker—now I won't have to tangle with his stupid ass." Bobby had a big grin on his face when he was telling me that, and I was pleased that Bobby realized that I could take care of myself if I had to.

One day on deck, Zeck was once again holding a short piece of line and trying to do something that I never quite understood. He walked up to me with his hand open. "You got your knife with you?" he asked. I reached into my pocket, pulled out the knife, and handed it to him. A couple of sailors saw what was happening and were watching anxiously. Zeck opened the knife, cut off a small length of his line, closed the knife, and then handed it back to me. "It's still very sharp," he said smiling, and I could tell he was just letting me know that he still respected my knife's cutting ability. I just smiled back at him and put the knife into my pocket, knowing that I would never again have to worry about Zeck. I also learned the same lesson my zadie Tzvi learned in Russia: there are times when you must stand up and be counted as a Jew, no matter what may happen afterward.

* * * *

My only disappointment in Bobby came when we went on a Mediterranean cruise that ended up in Naples, Italy. While in port at Naples, our fleet commander authorized three-day weekend passes for Catholic sailors who wanted to go to Rome and have a Sunday audience with the Pope in Saint Peter's Square. Bobby immediately applied for leave and was granted the weekend pass. He went to Rome by train with other Catholic sailors from our ship and a whole contingency from other ships in the sixth fleet, which was in Naples at that time. When he returned, he couldn't wait to show me what he had: two beautiful and I might add expensive-looking, rosaries. He was most pleased with himself and said boastfully, "I got these presents for Carmen and her mother." He waited while I admired them and said, "The best fuckin' thing about them is that when everyone was all gathered in Saint Peter's Square the holy-fuckin'-Pope came out and blessed us, which meant that anyone holding a fuckin' rosary had it blessed by the Pope too!"

The rosaries were made out of black and white stones that were exquisitely polished and the silver cross was very ornate and highly detailed. "Where did you get them?" I asked, since they looked much too expensive for Bobby's pocket.

Bobby said, all excited to tell me, that "Right outside of Saint Peter's Square there's a bunch of little souvenir stands that sold all kinds of fuckin' religious shit; so that's where I got em."

"Bobby, they look pretty expensive, what did you pay for them?" I asked, knowing Bobby was so broke that he had borrowed money just to pay for the trip to Rome. "How the hell did you buy them?"

"I fuckin' stole them," he said, surprised that I couldn't figure that out. "How the fuck else could I have gotten them?"

Needless to say, I was disappointed and tried to explain to Bobby, "You know Bobby, the Pope's blessing on the rosaries won't work because these rosaries weren't yours to have blessed. In fact, they won't ever really belong to Carmen or her mother because you stole the fuckin' things!" My voice was chastising and I tried to convey my sense of disappointment in Bobby.

He didn't understand what I was talking about. "Sure they're mine! I got 'em, don't I? And so what if they were stolen? They were stolen from some fuckin' wop—not an American. Hey, a few years ago the fuckin' wop probably would have shot me!"

When I pointed out that Bobby's wife and mother were of Italian descent, he just shrugged his shoulders. "Yeah, but they was never in Italy," he said as an explanation, still not seeing that what he had done was wrong. All I could think of at that time was that the catechism I taught him seems to answer fundamental questions about how one should use the knowledge they've gained for living together in the world. Bobby should have known that the eighth commandment, "Thou shalt not steal," applied to all things, not just items belonging to Americans, and that stealing from anyone was wrong!

I couldn't help but think that Sister Marie would be disappointed in me for not really teaching Bobby how to be a good Catholic. I just taught him enough by rote for him to pass a superficial test. By the same token, working with Bobby to teach him the catechism revealed to me that I did enjoy teaching. Even though I felt a sense of failure here in Italy, I probably still did him and his family some good. That said, I decided that if I ever taught anyone again, it wouldn't be to just memorize the words and parrot them back—obviously that wasn't what teaching and learning were all about. I met other sailors aboard ship whom I would teach things to, but in many cases it was the other sailors, that I would soon meet like William Pierce and Stephen Schroeder, who taught me how to learn and grow, and that proved to have the greater impact on my life.

After I left the ship, I never heard from Bobby again. I don't know if he ever got to corps school or if he stayed married or had a family, but I have to believe that I helped him survive beyond the navy and into his future civilian life. I think accepting him as a striker and teaching him basic first aid skills was good for Bobby's self image and gave him confidence to try things he thought he couldn't do before. I also feel that helping him become a Catholic and believing that he could be more than a deck ape was not all bad either. Bobby Johnson showed promise, and I have to believe that good things came from him.

Chapter 5

1952—William J. Pierce

William "Billy" Pierce was a sonarman and one of the first people I became friends with when I came aboard the *Bock*. A year older than me, Billy was married with a child; he was good looking, had a medium build and lots of black, wavy hair. Like Rocky Marciano, Billy grew up in Brockton, Massachusetts; Billy married his high-school sweetheart right after graduation, and started college in 1949. The couple had a son, William James Pierce, Jr.—or simply, Billy Jr.—early in 1950. At the time, Billy Sr. was finishing his first year in college where he was studying accounting for a career in banking. When the Korean War started in June of 1950 and the draft was reinitiated, Billy joined the navy rather than take his chances of getting drafted into the army and going off to Korea. Since he had some college and scored well on his placement tests, it was easy for him to get into sonar school in New London, Connecticut. After sonar school and a brief tour of duty on a training ship, Billy came aboard the *Bock* while it was getting re-commissioned in late 1951. I met him when I came onboard early in 1952. Billy talked like my friends from Chelsea—maybe a little classier—so it was easy for me to be comfortable with him. What was strange to me was that he was married and a father. I never had any friends close to my age who were married with children.

About a week after I arrived on the *Bock,* Billy came to sick bay and more formally introduced himself. He asked for some advice about his wife, who was being treated in Brockton for a minor hand injury. His easygoing attitude and openness with me about his family was refreshing, and it made me confident that I could handle my role as the ship's medical corpsman.

"Hey, doc! Can you help me out here?" he asked. "My wife, Barbara, was given some medicine." He looked at a piece of paper and spelled out the word "mafenide." "It's a cream from her doctor. She told me that she burnt the back of her hand, and it got infected." He said that Barbara had no idea what the drug was or what it was used for.

So I pulled out the few books I had, and the two of us went through them trying to locate the salve. We were also curious as to what other ailments it might be used for and why Barbara's doctor chose it. It was fun working with Billy like that. He was intelligent and apparently secure in doing a little medical research with me to figure out what was happening with his family. After locating Mafenide in *The Merck Manual* and reading its uses, we discussed why it seemed appropriate for Barbara's infection. We found that it was also used to combat gram-negative bacteria like gonorrhea. "You mean that if she caught the clap this stuff might cure it?" Billy joked. I smiled in response, but I didn't feel like I knew him well enough yet to make some wiseass joke about his wife's medical condition. In any case, it turned out that the infection was easily treated with the prescribed medication. Billy and I went out together later that evening in Boston where we found a pay phone for him to use to call home. He asked me to stay by him while he talked with Barbara about her infection.

"Honey, the doc here aboard ship tells me that salve the doctor gave you was just fine, but when you go back ask for a shot of penicillin, too. Also, hon, the doc says you should try to keep the sore covered when you're changing Billy's diaper, okay?"

*   *   *   *

After that first meeting Billy and I became buddies; we went on liberty together, drank together, went to the movies together, and just did all the things that close friends in the navy do. The one thing we didn't do together was getting laid; Billy always stayed faithful to Barbara.

Billy was interested in medicine and would frequently question me about things he had heard or read about, like the time during World War II when he heard about a corpsman—they were called pharmacist's mates (PM) then—

aboard a sub that performed an appendectomy at sea. Most corpsman had heard the story, and there was plenty of anecdotal information about the incident. As I remember hearing it, the PM was an OR tech at the naval hospital in Newport, Rhode Island, and was fascinated with gastrointestinal surgery. After his tour in Newport, he was assigned to independent duty aboard a submarine in the Pacific fleet. When subs went on a mission in wartime and a sailor became ill, it was highly unlikely that he would be transferred to a tender or shore-based facility. Apparently, prior to going on a combat mission, the PM had seen a crewman complaining of a dull, nonlocalized pain in his lower abdomen near his belly button. The pain tended to go to his right side, which is a classic appendicitis symptom. The PM suspected it might turn out to be a hot appendix, but he waited it out for a day. He knew that once they were out to sea, he wouldn't be able to get the seaman into a hospital and so would have to perform the appendectomy himself.

After another day out to sea and confirming with a blood count that the sailor's pain was indeed due to a hot appendix, the PM informed the captain of the medical emergency. He said that if the appendix burst and the seaman got peritonitis, he would in all likelihood die. The PM also told the captain that because of his OR experience, he could perform the appendectomy, safely taking out the infected appendix and saving the sailor's life. Knowing that there was no way to get the sailor to a better facility, the skipper gave the okay for the procedure and got the executive officer to act as anesthesiologist. He then made a boatswain's mate the surgical assistant because the petty officer had seen lots of action and wasn't queasy around blood.

The group prepped the sailor. Using the mess hall as an operating theater, the PM made a neat, clean McBurney's incision—the type of cut used when performing an appendectomy. He continued cutting down until he reached the peritoneum, as he had done many times before at Newport, except that now he went through the peritoneum layers and located the hot appendix, which looked just about ready to pop. He carefully tied it off and removed it. He quickly closed the incision and recovered the patient—something he had done many times before—and in about forty-five minutes the whole thing was over. When the war ended, word got out about the appendectomy, and much was made of the fact that navy PMs were so well trained that they could perform major surgery at sea, even in the cramped quarters of a Tambor-class submarine.

Billy was so impressed with this story that he had me teach him where and how a McBurney's incision was made and how an appendectomy was performed. He also made me promise that if I had to do such a procedure aboard the destroyer, he would get to be my assistant. I taught Billy other medical treatments, but our friendship was based on more than Billy's fascination with medicine.

✱   ✱   ✱   ✱

During a stay in Key West, Florida, I once got a two-day weekend pass to go to Miami. I was planning on visiting my aunt and uncle and their family. Billy, being the kind of friend he was, also got a pass and went with me. He was about the only person I knew at the time that I would ask to accompany me on such a visit. My family in Florida was from my mother's side—the Schwartz family—and they were a little different than my Detroit family on my father's side—the Rabins. I found the Schwartzes somewhat intimidating, and I rarely saw them unless they visited us in Detroit. My uncle was, at least in my eyes, a stiff and formal man. He was college educated and always seemed a bit pedantic to me and my family. I wasn't keen on going but I had promised my mother that I would visit them, so I did.

On the bus ride to Miami, I thought about my family's history and how my parents got together. I was told that my father, like his brother Mikie, had a good personality and was able to make a living as a salesman shortly after getting out of high school. He sold everything: pots and pans, jewelry, even insurance debit policies, which were life insurance policies that people paid off at a rate as low as ten cents a week. He was doing very well as a door-to-door salesman, with a personal list of customers who would buy almost anything he had to sell. As an independent salesman, my dad had very little overhead—just his brand-new, two-door Chevy Coupe ordered from the Dexter Chevrolet showroom; he also had enough money to keep him nicely dressed when he went to work. He was also able to eat lunch out, although Bubbie Mollie said no hamburgers: "You don't know what kind of chazzerei they put in there." He was a hard worker and earned enough money to occasionally go on dates. He also saved a little money and was still able to give his mother seven dollars a week for room and board. His parents didn't need the rent money, but as an adult out of school, it was the right thing to do in those days.

In 1928 dad got married to my mother, Ethel Schwartz—a dark-haired beauty, skinny like a flapper should be with a spit curl in the middle of her forehead. She was two years younger than my father, and some thought a little old not to have been married earlier. But my mother worked after high school as a stenographer and drove her own car, a rarity for women in those days, and was in no hurry to get married—that is, until my dad literally swept her off her feet with his dancing. Dad had learned to dance by watching his brother Mikie give dance lessons. After only a few dancing and movie dates, my parents decided to get married. Dad asked my mom's father, who owned the hardware store on Dexter, for her hand in marriage. I was told that he said, "Mr. Schwartz, Eta and I would like to get married, but before I give her a ring I would like your permission."

Mr. Schwartz liked Dad, and was impressed by his good manners in asking for his permission to get married. He knew our family, and said, "That's fine by me; you're a good boy, Sid, just take good care of our Eta and you should both be happy."

So my dad and Eta—my mom's Yiddish nickname—went to Plotnick the jeweler and picked out a diamond ring. Mr. Plotnick said, "Look Sid, I know that this one is more than you two wanted to spend now, but I also know in the long run it's a better deal for you. Take the ring and you can pay me off with whatever you can afford each month; no interest for you two; vigs are for the goyem." And so they got engaged. They were married in the summer of 1928 at Blumberg's Kosher Catering Hall on Dexter near Collingwood. One of the rabbis from the B'nai Moshe performed the service. After the wedding, they drove to South Haven, Michigan, on the shores of Lake Michigan for a five-day honeymoon at Sugarman's Lodge. Life was wonderful!

* * * *

When they returned to Detroit, they set up their home on the second floor of a well-kept, yellow-brick, four-story apartment building on Elmhurst and Lawton in the heart of the Jewish community. They had lots of items to furnish their new place with—some were newly purchased, some were wedding presents, and some were donated from their families, especially mom's very own double bed.

My mother continued to work at the brokerage house in downtown Detroit, while Dad continued with his sales work. As an independent salesman, he didn't work for a store or another person; whatever he wanted to sell he would take out on consignment from the wholesale houses on Twelfth Street near Clairmount. The area was a bustling commercial and residential area, with all kinds of wholesale distributors carrying jewelry, appliances, paper goods, pots and pans—just about anything one might want to sell door-to-door. Just like Dad's regular customers, the wholesalers all knew and trusted Dad. Some of the independent salesmen had to pay for their merchandise up front, but my dad always got his sales merchandise on consignment. Dad never sold a product he wouldn't buy himself, nor did he ever gouge anyone. He had one price for everyone no matter who you were—unless you were family, of course, and then you only paid what my dad paid.

Life looked good and Dad wanted to raise a family, but Mom was getting some bad feelings about the economy from her work at the brokerage firm. She wanted to wait for kids and kept telling my dad, "Sid, I'm scared. This economy looks like a 'house of cards' ready to collapse. Everyone is buying stock on borrowed money and sometime soon, I'm telling you, it's going to collapse." But nobody seemed to know this or care about it but her—and the stock market crash in the fall of 1929 proved her to be right.

The Wall Street crash hit everyone—Mom lost her job, and Dad's sales dropped off precipitously. Most of the independent salesmen he knew gave up their work for any kind of paying job because they needed cash. Dad was okay for a while because he was one of the few people at that time that had a savings account. The account was still active from his days of handling Uncle Mikie's dance lesson earnings, and he added the few dollars he was able to put away from his sales earnings. Consequently, Mom and Dad were able to get by on Dad's savings and by selling the occasional "hot ticket" item to his special customers. However, Dad was taking in significantly less money than he did before the crash.

Zadie Tzvi and Uncle Jack still ran the store, which they had expanded to include groceries and kosher meats. Like many small grocers at the time, they survived the crash because people still needed to eat. Being the kind of people they were, though, they gave away almost as much as they sold so that none of their customers would go hungry. This resulted in a serious loss of income for the family at the grocery store as well. Aunt Faye's husband was in the wholesale clothing business, which was also depressed, but like the rest of the family, they survived the worst of the Depression by sharing food, clothing, and other necessities. For years afterward, they would tell stories of how they survived with sadness, but more often than not, with much laughter.

"Remember that time when nobody had any cash and we were concerned about making our rent payment? Sid found a ten-dollar bill on the street in front of the store. We were like millionaires!" Mom would recall and everyone would chuckle and nod their heads. "Oy, were those some tough days," she would say.

* * * *

The Depression continued through the early thirties, but a new sense of hope surfaced when Franklin Delano Roosevelt was elected president. However, the old sense of despair over another war looming in Europe remained. Even though my parents weren't as prosperous as they would have liked, in 1932 they finally had their baby—me! I was their first and only child, and they named me Michael after my Uncle Mikie, just as Dad had promised. My middle name, Herbert, came from Mom's great-grandfather on the Schwartz side. I was born on a hot, summer day in June—some said it was the hottest summer in Detroit's history. My family referred to me as Little Michael at first but eventually started calling me Mike—not Mikie, because that was my uncle's nickname. Dad would correct anyone who mistakenly called me Mikie.

Although the Depression wasn't officially over, my parents no longer worried about surviving; they knew they could. Most of their friends and relatives were in the same situation, and those who needed it were helped out as much as possible by those who could afford it at the time. Life was hard but good; Bubbie Mollie still had the Pesach Seders at her house, and my Uncle Jack and Aunt Faye still lived in the neighborhood with their families. My grandparents' newest and last grandchild—me—had five older cousins to play with. I also had many other family members and friends to watch me grow up and hopefully become a respectable and honest member of the family. Those were comforting thoughts during my long bus ride up from Key West to Miami. I also had two older cousins from mom's sister but I really didn't know them all that well, and that's why I had some hesitancy in coming here to Miami.

* * * *

When our bus pulled into the station, I told Billy about my family in Miami that we would be meeting. "My mom's called Eta by the family, so if you hear them say Eta, you'll know they're talking about my mom," I explained. "Mom has only one sister here, my Aunt Lil, whose real name was Leila."

Billy was curious about Jewish families; he didn't know any Jews in Brockton or any now other than me, seeing as I was the only Jew aboard the ship. "Do all Jewish people have weird-sounding Yiddish names?" he asked.

"I guess most of us did," I said. "All the kids I went to Hebrew school with were called by their Yiddish names."

"What did they call you in Hebrew school?" he asked.

"Mikhail."

Billy smiled. "That sounds awfully close to Michael. How to you know they didn't fake it?"

I grinned at Billy and went on to tell him more about the Miami family. According to my mother, my Aunt Lil was seven years older than her and had been married to my Uncle Abe Solomon for over thirty years. "They had two daughters: my cousin Joanna, who they called Jen, was ten years older than me, and my cousin Miriam, or Mimi, was twelve years older than me." I also had to interject that Jen and Mimi were not Yiddish names—at least I didn't think they were. They were just typical, old-fashioned American nicknames.

"Mimi died in 1937 of cancer when she was just seventeen," I said. "I was just five when it happened, so I hardly remember her. The family remained in Detroit for a short time, but when my cousin Jen got married in 1940 they all moved to Miami. My uncle bought a drugstore with a lunch counter and took Jen's husband, Ernie, into the business with him."

It was a warm, sunny day, and we caught a local bus to an area where we knew they rented rooms by the day. We found lodging, got directions to my uncle's store, and caught a bus that ran up Biscayne Boulevard. I continued telling Billy about the family on the way to the store.

"My cousins Ernie and Jen were always really nice to me even though they were a lot older. They wrote to me once in a while and sent me gifts on my birthday and Hanukah. They also visited us when they came to Detroit. Cousin Ernie still had a lot of family there and came back almost every year to visit."

"Was Ernie his Jewish name?" Billy asked me facetiously, a silly grin on his face.

"Cut it out and pay attention," I said, pinching his cheek affectionately. "The reason my aunt and uncle had left Detroit was because their memories of Mimi were too painful—at least that's what my mother told me. Mimi's death was the main reason they moved to Florida, so they rarely came back to Detroit to visit."

I stopped telling Billy any more history, as he was obviously getting bored and overwhelmed with all the characters. He was paying more attention to what was happening outside the bus than to me. As the bus continued along the bright, clean Miami streets, I thought about the last time I heard from my mother. Upon hearing I was going to Key West, she had insisted that I be the first person in the family to visit my aunt and uncle in Miami. I also forgot to tell Billy that Ernie and Jen had two daughters since moving to Miami: Miriam, who was named after Mimi, was eleven, and Barbara was nine.

✱   ✱   ✱   ✱

I had called my uncle before we left our room and told him about how long I thought it would take us to get to the store. When we walked into my uncle's store on Biscayne Boulevard just south of the 79th street Causeway, which went over to all the fancy Miami Beach hotels on Collins Boulevard, my uncle was sitting at the counter waiting for us. He and Ernie were in the store, and my Aunt Lil was in the back doing some bookwork. Ernie was behind the lunch counter and insisted that Billy and I eat while we visited. They knew that we were there only Saturday and Sunday and didn't expect me to spend a lot of time with them, so they were going to make the most of our visit. They asked the usual "family visit" questions: "How's the family?" "What's the navy like?" "What are your plans after the navy?"

I answered each question as briefly as possible without being rude: "Everyone's fine." "The navy is okay; I'm learning a lot." "I'm planning on going to school when I get out."

After about an hour of visiting, my uncle called Ernie over and pointed to the caduceus on my sleeve. "Ernest, you see this? This is very, very important. It means that Mike has finally settled down and will probably go on to be a doctor and make us all very proud of him." Ernie just nodded and smiled knowingly, and then winked at me.

"Mike, what kind of cigarettes do you smoke?" my uncle asked.

"Phillip Morris," I answered and watched as took a carton from the shelf and gave it to me. I thanked him heartily. Smoking didn't nearly have the stigma in 1952 as it does today.

Ernie waited on some customers and then came back to where we were sitting. "Mimi's birthday party is today," he said. "Jen would love it if you could come and meet the girls."

Since I had actually never met them before, I was relieved to see that Billy's expression indicated he was fine with us going. "We'd love to come," I said. My aunt had an old 1939 Pontiac that still drove quite well, and after giving me directions on how to get to Ernie and Jen's place, she gave me the keys to her car and off we went. On the way over, I told Billy the girls' names and ages.

* * * *

When we arrived at Jen's place in the early afternoon—just in time for cake and ice cream—the party was well underway. About ten little girls attended the party, a lot of them dressed in pink for the special occasion. Most were Mimi's friends, naturally, but a couple of them were friends of Babs's—Barbara's nickname. I guessed that Ernie had called ahead and told Jen that two young sailors were on their way, although I'm sure the girls thought of us as older men. The girls started wildly shrieking and giggling at the sight of us showing up in our sparkling white uniforms, white hats, and black neckerchiefs. The girls were told that we would be coming to the party and they were obviously looking forward to meeting and talking to real sailors.

Billy was in his element. He talked with the kids, telling them about his wife and son and explaining what the sonarman insignia on his sleeve meant. He asked the kids their names what their favorite class in school was, teasing them at times and just smiling and being an all-around good guy. "No, you aren't just eleven, are you? I thought you were at least seventeen," he said, teasing one of the girls. I, on the other hand, was uncomfortable at first with all the attention. I really didn't connect well with kids, and I was anxious to just make the obligatory visit and then leave. But I watched Billy and soon was into it as well. My two younger cousins were thrilled that I was there and told everyone that I was their cousin, even though the girls already knew that. They sat close to me, and little Babs, who was a little on the chunky side, couldn't take her eyes off of me. She listened to everything I had to say and would repeat it for the girls who hadn't heard me.

"My cousin Mike is a doctor on a navy battleship. He keeps all the sailors well in case they have to fight." She said proudly to one of her invitees

Billy could play the piano so when he saw the piano in the front room he asked my cousin Jen if he could play, she said "That would be wonderful, I'm sure the girls would love it!"

"Well, I don't know if they'll love it but it might make them a little less noisy," he said. He was so much at ease with Jen and the girls that I just enjoyed watching him be him self.

Billy was playing all sorts of music, taking requests from the girls and singing along with them. I drifted over to the piano, sat down on his left side, and started in with "Heart and Soul." I thought it was a favorite party song that everyone knew how to play—well, almost everyone. We started in on the duet and in no time at all the girls wanted to learn Billy's part—the lyrical element. I played the rhythm side as Billy taught the girls the lyrics and music: "Heart and soul, I fell in love with you, heart and soul ..." Every now and then I would modify my part with a catchy little riff that Billy had taught me, and Cousin Babs would just laugh in delight over it.

As I began to get more comfortable with my role as older cousin, I realized that I was twenty years old now and no longer a teenager. Here I was with a married friend acting like an adult—that is, acting normal for a person my age. It was quite a revelation. The kids were having fun and we were having fun, and for the first time I guess I realized I was no longer a kid. I was moving into an older generation. I never thought about myself in that light before, and it was a slightly strange feeling, yet one I welcomed. By the time we had to leave, several hours later, I had truly bonded with my little cousins and felt like I'd known them all my life. My older cousin Jen was delighted that Billy and I came to the party. She said to us, "Mike, you and Billy were really sweet to show up here today and spend some of your time with the girls. I'm glad you finally got to meet them!" She gave me a big hug, and then said, "Well Michael, I hope you enjoyed the girls company as well. I know that Mimi will be talking about this party for a long time to come." She had a big smile on her face, and hugged me once again, and then she hugged Billy.

We were all smiles and hugs. Both of the girls hugged and kissed us good-bye and Babs said in a gently pleading voice, "Mike, Mike ... I promise to write to you, will you write to me?"

I answered, "Babs, honey, I promise to write you back from anywhere in the world, okay?" And so Billy and I left with grins on our faces and warmth in our hearts for being able to attend an eleven-year-old's birthday party and to have had such a good time.

*　　*　　*　　*

When we got back to my uncle's shop to return my aunt's car, they had all heard what a success we were at the party. My uncle, in his own formal way said, "Thank you, Michael for visiting us old folks and for bringing such an intelligent and talented friend with you," as he looked over to Billy, to which Billy just smiled.

My Aunt Lil said, "I just talked to Mimi on the phone. We just hung-up a little while ago and Mimi couldn't stop talking about you. She told me how your friend Bill played piano for them, and she said he sang with them, and talked to all her friends. And Babs sounded truly smitten with her cousin Mike and said she can't wait to see you again." Aunt Lil was very excited and actually gushing over us; I had never seen her that way before. Then Aunt Lil reminded me that Mimi was named after Jen's sister, Miriam. She asked, "Mike do you remember your cousin Miriam? I know she was a lot older than you."

I said, "Of course I do, Aunt Lil," and her eyes welled up with tears. "I was really little, but I can still picture her in your apartment on Tuxedo near Linwood. You had that giant frog pillow that I would play with." In reality, I remembered their apartment well but vaguely remembered Miriam. However, I knew it would please my aunt if I told her that I remembered Miriam. I guess that's part of no longer being a teenager: making your older relatives happy to see you and being responsive to their needs. We left with much fanfare—hugs and kisses all around. Uncle Abe hugged me and gently slipped me a ten-dollar bill. "That's for you and your friend's dinner," he said quietly.

"Come back and visit any time," Aunt Lil said warmly. "And you're welcome to use my old Pontiac again."

"Keep safe and enjoy the rest of your time in Miami," Uncle Abe added. I thanked them again for the cigarettes and everything else, and then we walked out to catch the bus back to our room. As we were walking to the bus-stop and out of sight from the store I told Billy about the ten spot my uncle gave me for our dinner, and Billy was thrilled. "We're going to have a good dinner tonight—maybe even filet mignons! What do you say Mike, my friend?"

We cleaned up and went out for that good dinner early that evening; it was beef filets and roast potatoes. After dinner we were wandering around Miami where the evening had cooled off, the sky was clear and the smell from the soft ocean breeze was very pleasant. While walking I began to hear an accordion playing "Evenin' Time" ("A couple of stars are shining now, its evenin' time ...") and we ran into the Art Van Damme Quintet's lounge. It was a quiet, comfortable place—dark wood and leather—with not many customers then, so we wandered in and spent the rest of the night listening to the group and drinking gin rickys. We talked about the day, and Billy told me, "You know Mike, I really had a good time. It was like being with family again and best of all we are off of that ugly fucking ship. I really enjoyed meeting your cousins and your aunt and uncle, they're very nice people," to which I had to agree. Billy continued, "I'm surprised you did so well with the kids. I didn't think you could spend that much time with kids and enjoy yourself."

"What makes you think I enjoyed myself? What kind of asshole do you take me for going to baby's birthday parties?" I said in mock anger. But I liked it when

Billy told me I had changed—maybe not in those words—but it meant that he saw that I was growing up and acting more mature.

* * * *

A few months after we got back from Key West and were permanently stationed in Norfolk, Virginia, Billy told me that he was having a problem. It seems that he was losing his hair in some spots on his scalp, and it was beginning to worry him. I examined him as best I could and saw no unusual scaling or other symptoms of skin disease, so we took out the trusty *Merck Manual* and looked up his symptoms. We found that his condition seemed to fit the description for alopecia areata, a type baldness not associated with the more typical male pattern baldness. I filled out a hospital referral chit and wrote in the diagnosis box, "DU alopecia areata." The DU in front of the diagnosis stood for "diagnosis undetermined," since corpsmen were not allowed to diagnose illnesses. I sent Billy over to see the doctor on the tender. When he returned a few hours later, I saw that on my referral chit the doctor had written "alopecia." He had sent Billy back with some antiseptic shampoo, which he directed Billy to use every time he showered, preferably every day. Now I knew that *The Merck Manual* said there was no known satisfactory therapy for alopecia, so the shampoo the doctor had given Billy made me doubt his competence. Maybe the doctor thought Billy's condition was psychological and that by giving him something resembling a treatment it would clear it up. It didn't.

Billy continued to lose his hair in small clumps. Sometimes some of his hair would grow back, but then other clumps would appear. So Billy shaved his head because he felt funny with the patches of baldness and thought a shaved head looked better. I could see that the experience was depressing Billy; his good-natured personality was becoming gloomy and he seemed pensive. Once, when we were just sitting around bullshitting about our lives, Billy told me that he was worried about the future. "You know, Mike, Barbara and Billy Jr. are still living with my parents, which is hard for them," he confessed. "I've been trying to save for school when I get out, but now I'm beginning to look like some kind of freak, and I haven't saved nearly enough to go back to college."

I knew that something wasn't right with my friend. When I heard that the *Bock* was going to the naval base in Charleston, South Carolina, to load ammunition in the late fall of 1952, I came up with an idea on how to get Billy some better medical treatment. I knew that it would create a stir if I tried to bypass the tender doctors in Norfolk, so I told Billy that I was going to send him over to the naval hospital in Charleston. "It has to be for an emergency medical condition," I explained. "When we're in Charleston, I'll fill out a chit with a new diagnosis: DU depressive illness. I'll indicate on the form that you've been upset since your onset of alopecia and have recently been talking of suicide."

It was a little risky, but Billy agreed that it wouldn't hurt to see someone who might be more knowledgeable than that asshole doctor from the tender. Billy also confided that he *was* thinking about killing himself, although he said that he would never actually do it. Lots of sailors talk about killing themselves from time to time, so I didn't jump off my chair when he told me that, but I was even more concerned than before.

The November sky was overcast and gray when we anchored at the ammo depot upriver from Charleston. It was so cold that you could see an occasional snowflake in the air, which was quite unusual for Charleston at that time of year. I got permission to escort Billy in the launch over to the naval base, where I arranged for his transportation to the hospital. Then I shook Billy's hand and watched him leave on an old battleship-gray bus.

Billy didn't return to our ship during the two days we were there loading ammo. When we returned to Norfolk, I still hadn't heard anything from him. I notified the exec that I sent Sonarman Third Pierce to Charleston Naval Hospital and had not heard from him or the hospital since. A day later the exec had some of the other sonarmen pack up Billy's things to ship to the naval hospital. The exec told me later that the hospital staff had informed him that Billy had been admitted to Charleston with both psychological and physical problems and was being treated, but he was not expected to return to the *Bock*. I felt some relief for Billy but more anxiety than anything else. I wondered what was wrong with him and what were they going to do with him and whether his family knew. A few days later, I was able to get to a pay phone and call the hospital. I told them I was Sonarman Pierce's corpsman from the *Bock* and was inquiring about his status. They soon connected me to his ward, where the ward nurse surprised me by asking if I wanted to talk to Pierce. "Yes, I do!" I said immediately.

Billy got on the phone and said, "Hey Mike! How you doin? I'm doin just fine here, the doctors here are great. They told me that this type of alopecia could be caused by emotional stress and that suicide, or at least thoughts of suicide, were not uncommon under the circumstances, so you see, I'm normal!"

"That's good to hear—so you're finally normal." I said that to add some levity to the conversation.

Billy went on to say, "Hey, the real good news is that this alopecia shit is heavy duty, so they're going to give me an early discharge—medical, under honorable conditions! Not a section eight! I have to go for some more counseling and interviews, but I might even be home by Christmas; well maybe I'll be home by then." He sounded great, like his old good-natured self again, and I was relieved that it all seemed to be working out for him. Early in 1953, Billy got his honorable, medical discharge with no stigma attached and went home to Brockton. He returned to college in the spring term and seemed by all accounts to be very happy.

* * * *

I kept in touch with Billy both by phone and letter. In the fall of 1953, I was assigned to Quonset Point, Rhode Island, and Billy invited me up to Brockton to spend a Sunday with him and his family. I finally got to meet Barbara, Billy Jr., and Billy's parents, in what I believed to be a very typical New England family setting. The leaves were just beginning to change and Billy's house was a very typical New England style clapboard house, built sometime towards the end of the nineteenth century. It was two stories with shuttered windows on an old street in a middle-class neighborhood of Brockton. Billy's family said that they were all pleased to meet me. They had heard many stories about the times we spent together—like our trip to Miami and my cousin's birthday party.

Billy looked great—his hair was mostly grown back, and the few small patches of baldness were hardly noticeable under all his other wavy, black hair. I found out that Barbara was a couple of months' pregnant; nobody knew it except them and now me. They were going to wait awhile before surprising the family. And Billy Jr. was a real cutie at three years old, just starting to talk in full sentences. "Pleased to meet you Uncle Mike," he said when we were introduced. You could see his father in him, but he also had his mother's charm and good looks. I was also impressed at how well behaved he was; no tantrums, yelling or rowdy behavior.

Billy was showing me around his parent's big, old home and wanted me to see the room that he, Barbara, and Billy Jr. shared. He was telling me about a corpsman he met at the Charleston Naval Hospital in South Carolina. "You know, Mike, before I got discharged I had to go to psych rehab. The rehab corpsman there was an HM3 about your age, and I asked him if he knew you—I mean, why not ask? Well, he said he did. He said you and him were in corps school together."

"No shit!" I said. "Do you remember his name?"

"No, but he certainly knew you," Billy said. "We shared a number of Mike Rabin stories and—you'll get a kick out of this—he told me that he once bet you that you couldn't remember or spell that medical compound for Salvarsan."

"Oh yeah, I remember him! What was his name? Was it Ben?"

"I don't remember his name either, but I asked him for a piece of paper when he told me the story of the bet. I wrote out that damn fifty-four-letter word and said, 'do you mean this?' He just about cracked up!"

Billy and I were laughing so hard that Barbara thought something was wrong and came in to see if we were both all right. When she saw that we were just laughing, she smiled and left. I forgot that I had told Billy all about Bobby Johnson finding the word in the *Hospital Corps Handbook* and what I did—wrote it out—when Bobby asked me about the drug.

Billy thought that story was so great, even though a bit cruel, that he wanted to see the drug and learn it for himself. And there at the Charleston Naval Hospital was Billy's chance to use that little bit of worthless information. What a thrill for him, and what a great story for me.

The rest of the day was just delightful—dinner, talking, family, TV—in some sense it was just like being home again, only now I was an adult in an adult's home (even though Billy shared it with his parents). The feeling of seeing my friend in a normal home situation; being a civilian again was very nice, indeed.

On the way back to Quonset Point, I reflected on the day I spent with Billy's family. He was a civilian now, and I was out there visiting with him in the civilian world—not some cruddy naval base. The fighting war in Korea had ended in July, and servicemen and women were returning from around the world. I still had another year of service to go, but college and civilian life were on my mind. Visiting with Billy showed me what that life might be like—contented, happy, a family of my own and the chance for a good future. But I must admit that what I thought about most on the trip back to Quonset Point was what a fine ass Barbara Pierce had.

CHAPTER 6

1953—CHARLIE THE GHOST

We were just about to pull into Plymouth, England, for a three-day visit to load stores and give the crew some well-deserved R&R when the executive officer came in to sick bay. Mr. Miniard—the crew referred to him as "Minnie" but not to his face—informed me that I was just "volunteered" for three days of medical shore patrol. I was furious. We had started out on a Mediterranean cruise late in March of 1953, and the ship had already spent a few weeks doing various military exercises in the North Atlantic and visiting Londonderry, Ireland. After Plymouth we were to sail to Cannes and Nice, France, and finally end up in Naples, Italy, before returning to Norfolk, Virginia. I found out a couple of days before that I had made HM2, and had the ship's tailor, who was also our laundryman, sew on my new stripes. I was admiring my jumper when the exec gave me the news about my shore patrol assignment.

Lieutenant Commander Miniard was a tall, stocky, middle-aged mustang who was well liked by the enlisted men, including me. He was a sailor's officer in the sense that he had been an EM, which enabled him to understand our feelings and know how to talk to us. He was tough, unafraid of giving orders, and most of all, fair. It was not unusual for him to stop by sick bay and talk with me or the other sailors that might be there. He always wanted to know how the men were and if anyone was sick. So when he stopped by and asked, "Hey Rabin, anybody sick today?" it was always reassuring that Minnie was there for us.

I said, "Not today sir; the crew's too excited about going into Plymouth." My voice was excited because I had made plans to go in later in the day with some friends.

It was right after that when Minnie told me, "Oh, by the way, I volunteered you for medical shore patrol duty for the three days we're in port." He sounded happy about it, like it was some kind of nice thing to do for me, but I was less than happy—and I respectfully let him know that.

"For all three days? Don't you think that's a bit too much, sir?" I said, with obvious disappointment in my voice.

He didn't apologize nor change my duty assignment but quietly explained, "You'll live off the ship at a local bed and breakfast and receive ComRats while on your duty assignment." ComRats meant I would get extra money for meals and the B&B expenses. Minnie went on to say, "And you'll be stationed at the British Shore Patrol headquarters in Plymouth. You'll have more than enough time to do as you please and I thought you'd like this assignment." He seemed to think he was doing me a favor—which, as it turned out, he was.

I packed my ditty bag for two nights and three days and went off in to Plymouth to report for duty at the British Shore Patrol headquarters. The shore patrol was housed in a police station—or gaol, in Brit talk—that I guessed was at least two hundred years old. The building was given over to the military during World War II as a short-stay prison (essentially a brig) and as headquarters for both the military police and shore patrol. It was still used as a brig, as Plymouth was a busy seaport that saw many sailors from the United Kingdom and a host of other countries make port there. In fact, our entire destroyer squadron was in town, along with Canada's only operational aircraft carrier at that time. So Plymouth was busy with sailors, many of whom would likely be getting into typical sailor troubles. Some would probably participate in fights, drunken rowdiness, prostitute harassment, and other such activities that sailors often engaged in when visiting a friendly country. Bad behavior was even more common when sailors were coming in to port after having spent some time at sea. As a result, the Brits required that large contingencies of foreign ships coming into port had to have their own medical personnel stationed at the brig to take care of their sailors who might get injured or sick on liberty—even sailors like us Yanks.

*   *   *   *

SP headquarters looked like an old, gray brick fort. It was two stories high but with the circular towers on the side of the front entrance and an odd looking attic window right in the middle, just above the second story, it appeared a lot taller, and I might add, just a bit creepy. I went in and met some of the British military personnel stationed there. I was pleasantly surprised to meet another U.S. Navy corpsman from one of the other ships who had also just arrived for a three-day medical SP tour of duty—a nice guy named Al who was from somewhere in Minnesota. Al told me that he started college before joining the navy and was planning to finish his undergraduate degree when his four-year tour of duty was up. We got along well and spent most of our days visiting places in the city and eating nice meals on our ComRats allowance. In the evenings we had some busy times, but for the most part the British and American SPs kept things from getting out of hand. None of the sailors brought in while we were there needed any serious medical care, such as stitches or casts. They usually required only some minor first aid and a place to sleep it off.

Plymouth was a quaint and storied city that was surrounded by sailing and naval history. Most of the buildings, including the houses, looked to be around the same age as the gaol, so it wasn't a very modern-looking community. Nevertheless, after the war Plymouth had developed a modern waterfront park off of some low-lying cliffs away from the port. The beach area was rather small in depth and the shallow cliffs rose rapidly behind the beach. In order to have more park area, they terraced the cliff in the center so as to have three different levels; playgrounds at the top, beaches on the bottom, and picnic areas, in the center; it was just spectacular. When Al and I went exploring, we found the beach area by accident and were amazed at all the people in bathing suits and summer dress. It may have been sunny and pleasant out, but we both thought, with temperatures only in the sixties, that it was still a little too cool for bathing suits. It was no surprise that we didn't see anybody in the cold Atlantic waters actually swimming.

When Al and I returned to the brig, from our early afternoon exploration of Plymouth, the Brits took us on a quick tour of the old facility. They called it a "cook's tour" because it was actually conducted by their navy cook, whom we were told had been there the longest. They also called it a cook's tour to play on the famous Thomas Cook travel agency tours. The layout of the facility was interesting but I guess it was typical for eighteenth-century British gaols. The main first-floor office area had been divided into four rather large spaces that were furnished more like an old manor house than a former prison. Each of these large rooms had a fireplace or stove that burned coal. Like most of England at that time, the gaol had no central heating. The weather was fairly mild during our April visit, so we never had any need for daytime heating. The reason why I'm going into such detail about all the heating arrangements in the brig will become clear soon enough.

Al and I were assigned to the smallest of the four rooms on the first floor, which we discovered cooled off in the evenings and could get uncomfortably cold at night. The other three larger rooms were for British military use. One large room was a general working and meeting area for muster, getting assignments, and the like. Another smaller room was reserved for the duty officers. The last and largest room was the EM's mess hall and common room, where tea was always available and meals were served to the British crew. The duty officers' room occasionally had a fire going at night if someone would request it. The larger meeting area used for muster was also where the on-duty EM staff hung out. That room also occasionally had a fire at night. There was a coal-burning stove in the mess hall, but I never saw it in use while we were there. The separate sleeping quarters and washrooms for the officers and the enlisted men took up the entire second floor.

The prisoners' quarters were located along three cell blocks on a split lower level, about six steps down from the main building's first floor. You could get to the prison quarters directly from the left wing of the main building. You could also step down from the exit in the mess hall through a heavy wrought iron gate and then into a small, enclosed courtyard. The square courtyard was formed by the main building and the cell blocks all arranged at right angles to one another. Two of the cell blocks were connected by a passageway at one corner. Each block contained a bank of prison cells. The third block ran from the right wing of the main building and joined up with the other two cell blocks at the opposite corner.

The only access to the third block was from the main building's right wing, and a door from the courtyard. The third block held only a few rooms for storing heating supplies and food. There may have been ten prison cells in the first two blocks, maybe four or five in each—at best, it was sparsely populated. Each cell had a bench, toilet without a seat, a very small sink, one light bulb from the ceiling, no windows, and a steel door with a small, screen-covered viewing window in it. Although the cells had no visible signs of heating arrangements, the Brits apparently never questioned the fact that it could get cold at night. I guess that's the way things were supposed to be in a British prison—uncomfortable.

You could see that the gaol wasn't meant to hold prisoners for more than one or two nights. During the day, the prison cell blocks were essentially empty. However, by late evening drunken or disruptive sailors started coming in, and by midnight, when most sailors had to be back to their ships, as many as four or five cells might be in use.

*   *   *   *

When American sailors were brought in, Al and I were asked to check on them to make sure that they weren't injured or too sick to stay there for the night. As it turned out, we never really had to treat anyone for anything other than minor cuts and abrasions suffered in fights or from resisting arrest. Most detainees would just pass out on the bench or floor and sleep it off till morning when they were released. When they returned to their ships, they were put on report for being AWOL because being in the brig was no excuse. As a result, besides spending the night in jail, the poor, hungover sailors usually had to appear before a disciplinary captain's mast. As for us corpsmen, though, it was a relatively easy assignment. It would seem that Minnie was right: I had more time to visit places, eat well, and—best of all—enjoy a couple of nights in my own private bedroom.

On the first night of duty, I agreed to stay at the prison till at least midnight when all liberties were up and any one needing medical care was treated. Al and I agreed to take turns staying late, and we knew that whoever stayed the first night got the last night, too, which was fine with me. Later that first night, one of the British SPs invited me down to the cell block to see how the prisoners were being housed and how the Brits treated their prisoners; there were no Americans for me to see at that time.

Only two cells were occupied in the first cell block, and none were occupied in the second block. The two cells being used were widely separated. In one of those cells, the lone prisoner inside was carrying on something fierce. He was a British seaman who was obviously drunk and acting disorderly: yelling, swearing, pounding on the door, and doing everything possible to create a noisy and fractious scene. The sailor in the other cell, also a British seaman, was passed out on a bench and so was unperturbed by the raucousness down the corridor.

"Do you wanna see how I quiet these guys down?" the SP asked me with a serious look on his face. Not knowing exactly what he meant by "quiet down," I agreed.

The SP went up to the window in the door and yelled at the drunk. "Look here, you! Either quiet down now or I'll leave, turn off the fuckin' lights, and let

Charlie quiet you down." With that, the SP turned off the light in the cell and the corridor lights near it. Within seconds the previously very noisy drunk was pleading—in tears—not to let Charlie get him.

"Please, please, I beg of you! Turn the fuggin' lights back on!" he slurred with obvious tears in his voice. The SP waited a few moments until the prisoner had quieted down, with the exception of some whimpering, and then turned on the lights.

"Now, you gonna behave?" the SP asked.

"Yeah, yeah, I will, I will," the drunk said, now sounding very sober.

"Who the hell is Charlie?" I asked in amazement, thinking it must be some kind of nickname for a form of punishment, like a whip or something else that the Brits still practiced in their navy.

"Why, Charlie's our bloody ghost," he answered with a straight face.

Thinking at first that he was joking or that this was some kind of a local practice used to frighten drunks and dumb sailors, I asked for more details. The SP then told me the story of Charlie the ghost and how his presence around the brig was well-known in Plymouth, especially to the sailors stationed there.

"When this ere fuckin' brig was the Plymouth gaol, the layout was pretty much like you see it now, only those cell blocks were modernized just prior to World War II," he explained. "But before the bloody military took it over, it was actually used as a long-term prison, and they hung the poor fuckers that were convicted and sentenced to die." Without a pause, he continued, "Some of the bloody cells in the third block were originally part of death row. You see, those are accessible only from the courtyard or the main building, but now they're just used as storage cellars."

I thought about my cook's tour earlier in the day and recalled the arrangement of the rooms along the third cell block's corridor. As we sat there on the bench in the corridor the SP quietly continued his explanation of Charlie the ghost. "The last three rooms in that fuckin' block were for the condemned prisoners. They're smaller in size than the modern cells you see here," he said, pointing to the cells in the block we were in. "Now that strange, small, circular looking room at the end of the corridor was the cell reserved for the prisoner who was to be hanged the next morning. He was placed there so he couldn't hurt himself on his last night. Did you see earlier that that's where we keep the bloody coal?"

I nodded. "I assumed that the coal stored there fed all the fireplaces and stoves when it was cold," I said.

He went on to ask, "Did they show you the two little rooms next to that cell?" Again, I nodded. "Well, that first little room next to the bloody condemned man's cell originally held the lye pit. That's where the dead bodies of the prisoners were tossed to rot after they were hung in the courtyard. I expect that you saw that the old lye pit had been filled in. Did you see that the room now holds the kindling wood and newspapers that we use to start the coal fires?"

My throat felt too dry to answer, so again I just nodded. "The little storage cellar next to the lye pit room was where a condemned prisoner was billeted until just before his last night," he said quite seriously. "The condemned prisoner would be taken from that last bloody hemispherical cell out to the courtyard at sunrise on the day that his sentence was to be carried out. Then he would be executed by hanging, and after he was dead, they threw him into the bloody lye pit."

We paused in silence, while we both lit up cigarettes—I offered him one of mine—and started to smoke. Finally, I asked, "So who was Charlie?"

"Well, we think that Charlie—that's the bloody name we gave the poor fucker—was the last one executed. We think that he just bloody hell refuses to leave the fuckin' place."

I didn't ask why the prisoners weren't buried but were just thrown into the lye pit. I assumed that most were probably poor and without any family who could give them a proper religious burial.

* * * *

I must admit that the seriousness with which the SP told me Charlie's story put a chill in my spine. It also made me a little uncomfortable because I had had a bizarre experience in our duty room earlier that evening. When I was just settling into our assigned quarters, a young British seaman came in while it was still light out and asked in a very obsequious voice, "Do you need your coal bucket filled or would you be wanting any kindling for starting a fire later in the evening?"

It was still warm, and I wasn't sure that I would need a fire. "You needn't bother," I said. "If I want any coal and stuff, I'll just get it later." I knew from our cook's tour earlier in the day where the fire supplies were located.

The young kid looked at me anxiously. "You mean you would get them after dark?" I was a bit taken aback by his frightened expression, but I thought that maybe he was a little out of it or that British seamen were far more deferential to petty officers than American sailors.

He left with a concerned look on his face and then returned shortly with a flashlight. "Here's a torch," he said. "There are no lights in those supply rooms. The corridor is pretty dim, too, so if you really plan on getting fire supplies later, definitely take the torch." He turned it on and off to make certain it worked and then left it there for me.

As it turned out, after it got dark but before I was invited to see how the prisoners were treated, it did get chilly. I decided to make a fire to warm up a bit, but more for just having something to do. I took the torch, went into the mess hall, out the back door and then through the large iron gate and down the few stairs into the courtyard. The courtyard was dimly lit by the light coming in from the windows and the doorway in the main building. I walked over to the third cell-block entrance, which was in a dark corner off to my right at the rear of the courtyard. The door was located in front of the strange circular room. I went in and found that the corridor was, indeed, faintly lit. Only a couple of low-wattage bulbs appeared in the ceiling, and they were at the opposite end where the entrance to the main building wing was located.

So with my torch lit, I opened the door to the coal room—the former condemned man's cell, although I didn't know it at that time—and there stacked quite high and filling most of the room was the coal pile. Next to the door was a shovel, which I used to fill my coal bucket. I then went next door—the old lye pit room—and placed some paper and kindling wood in my bucket. After closing the door, I left the block through the courtyard entrance and went back to the duty room and started a fire. I was quite pleased with myself, being a Yank and living in what I thought to be a very British way. After hearing the story about Charlie, I understood the expression on the young sailor's face and it made the hairs on my neck stand up.

I left the prison after midnight and found my way back to the B&B where I was lodging. The B&B was not far from the prison. It was in an old three-story house with old-fashioned furniture and even older lighting and plumbing; I think the Brits might have called it quaint, but at that moment I found it scary. The older neighborhood that housed the B&B wasn't well lit or heavily populated, especially at night. I found that walking alone after midnight was a little disconcerting that night, to say the least.

* * * *

The next morning, I went down for breakfast and the friendly B&B owner asked how my first day at the prison went. I told her it was interesting but for the most part uneventful.

"Well then, did you meet up with Charlie?" she asked.

I was taken aback by the casualness of her comment. When I told her about the drunken sailor being sobered by the threat of Charlie coming to visit him, she wasn't at all surprised.

"Yeah, he's well-known for sobering a lot of sailors in his day." She didn't act like Charlie was just a local joke that shouldn't be taken seriously.

When I got to the brig after breakfast, Al was already there. I couldn't wait to tell him all about Charlie and the prisoner, my landlady's remarks, and the frightened young seaman. We were in our little room and Al was sitting by the fireplace when I came in. When I started telling Al about Charlie he was totally taken in by the story and was very excited. He stood up and started pacing as I told him the whole story; then he said, "My God! Shit! Think about it—we're staying in a fuckin' haunted prison!"

We went over to the mess hall to get some tea and found a few British sailors hanging around in there. The cook had made us some coffee. We appreciated the gesture, and thanked them, of course, but the coffee tasted really bad. The cook brewed it like tea, by just throwing the coffee grinds in some tepid water.

As we conversed with the Brits in the mess hall, one of them asked, "Which one of you went down after dark to get coal?" I guess the word about the crazy American sailor had gotten out.

When I admitted that it was me, the Brit smirked and said, "Well, did Charlie bother you?"

The other sailors were watching with great interest. I said, in what I thought was an obvious joking manner, "Oh yes—we had a brilliant conversation and a spot of tea over in the old lye pit room."

Looks of incredulity and disdain covered the sailors' faces. Clearly, they neither appreciated my British affectation nor my joking about Charlie. I should point out that in those days British sailors often affected American accents when talking with us, which I didn't appreciate either. So I understood their feelings but was put off by their reaction anyway.

Al and I went back to our office and talked a little more about Charlie and what his story might really mean; was it simply British superstition or was he real? A short time later, a trim-looking, young British naval officer came into our office. In a stiff, commanding way he told us smartly to remove our feet from the fireplace hearth. He said, "Take your shoes off the hearth; we clean that, you know," and we immediately put our feet down and stood up. He then inquired, "So, how are you chaps getting along; are the arrangements here to your satisfaction?"

We remained standing almost at attention and replied, "Yes, sir; everything is fine, and thanks for your hospitality, we really appreciated the coffee." He nodded his approval and looked around the room with his hands smartly clasped behind his back. I then asked in a respectful but skeptical voice, "Sir, would you please explain the story we heard about Charlie the ghost?"

"It's no joke. He's there, you know," he replied quite seriously and then abruptly left. With open mouths Al and I looked at each other. We didn't know whether to laugh or be terrified.

*   *   *   *

I offered to spend the second night at the gaol because Al wanted to meet with some friends from his ship that night, which meant that he would pull the last late-night duty. It was still early in the evening when we returned from dinner, and I sent Al off to visit with his buddies. Since it was still light out, I decided to take the opportunity to fill the coal bucket; I wasn't sure whether the young seaman would be around later offering to fill the bucket again. As I went down to the death row cell block, I was a bit nervous but wasn't about to let the Brits think I was afraid to go there in the daylight.

When I went into the former condemned man's cell, the strange circular one where the coal was stored, I couldn't find the shovel. I walked halfway around the coal pile with my torch and then found it on the other side of the room on the floor next to the wall. I picked it up, walked back around to the open door, and filled the bucket. Not wanting the Brits to think I was a slob, I carefully put the shovel back against the wall by the door, just as I did the previous night. Then I got some paper and kindling from the old lye pit room and went back to our office.

It was just getting toward evening, so I went over to the mess hall to get some coffee or tea and discovered a small group of British sailors standing around and talking. One was speaking in a perfect American Midwestern accent, just like mine, and the others were listening attentively to what he was saying. I thought for sure that they were mocking me. I moved closer to listen when I noticed that the American-sounding Brit was wearing a hat with the ship name "Magnificent"—the Canadian carrier's name. Canadian sailors dressed just like British sailors, and until I saw his hat I was certain he was a Brit. I asked where he was from, and he told me Windsor, Ontario, which is located right across the river from Detroit; no wonder why he sounded like me. We had a delightfully animated conversation about the places we both frequented in Windsor and

Detroit—mostly restaurants and movies in Detroit and nightclubs in Windsor. The legal drinking age in Windsor was only eighteen and they frequently didn't ask for IDs. The Brits seemed to enjoy the fact that we had both come all this way to meet up here and then find out that we were essentially neighbors.

The conversation slowly drifted over to Plymouth and then to Charlie. The Canadian was just as surprised as I had been to hear about a ghost in the prison. I was careful to keep my tone serious yet somewhat inquisitive as I asked just how much the Brits knew about Charlie. They all offered their own personal stories about Charlie's manifestations.

"Sometimes when I go out into the courtyard to get into the other storage cellars, Charlie will close the bloody courtyard gate," the cook said. "I would have to put down any stores I would be carrying back so I could open the gate."

I knew there was no way that wrought iron gate could close by itself, even in a strong wind. Others told of similar events: closing doors, switching lights on in the corridor at night when no one was there. It seemed that in general, Charlie never did any real harm but was more or less just being a prankster. The Canadian seemed impressed by the stories, and we both thanked the Brits for sharing their ghost legends with us. The Canadian sailor and I exchanged names and addresses. We wished each other a safe voyage home and promised to meet up someday in Windsor for a night out after our tours of duty were up.

Later when I was alone in the office, I began to reflect on Charlie's purported activities. I started to think how I had felt so strange getting coal earlier that day. Then I recalled that I had found the coal shovel halfway around the room on the other side of the coal pile. I also realized that no one had been in the coal storage room because it had been too early for the young seaman to fill the coal buckets. Now if I was the last one in the coal room last night, which seemed obvious, then how did the shovel get to the other side of the room? The only possibility was that someone carried it away from where it was placed against the wall near the door. Then the person would have had to walk halfway around the heaped up pile of coal and grime to dump it—in the dark, unless the person had a torch like mine. The person also could have heaved the shovel over the top of the coal pile from the entryway to get it to the other side of the room. I knew I didn't do that because I remembered exactly how I placed the shovel by the door the night before. So how did the shovel get there? Charlie! It was the only logical answer.

* * * *

There was little talk of Charlie on our last day of SP, but I did tell Al about how I found the shovel way over on the other side of the room. He shook his head in disbelief and said, "Well, as soon after midnight as I can I'm leaving this weird place. And I don't give a shit how cold it might get I'm not making any kind of fire." He was half joking when he spoke, but you could tell that he was also serious about leaving as soon as he was no longer needed.

When I returned to my ship that evening after my last ComRats dinner, I didn't say anything to anyone about my shore patrol experience. But the next afternoon when we were out to sea again and a few of us were sitting on the fantail talking about our time in Plymouth, I told my story about Charlie the ghost. I made certain that they fully understood the experience I had with the shovel and that it only could have been Charlie who moved it around.

"Bullshit," was a response from one of my more eloquent shipmates. "There's no such things as fuckin' ghosts."

But then another one of my shipmates, whom we affectionately called Numb-Nuts (don't ask) spoke up. "Well, I believe it! Shit, that's the trouble with most Americans. They don't believe shit, and that's why we don't have no fuckin' ghosts—the fuckin' limeys got 'em all. Maybe if we believed then we could have ghosts, too. What do you think, Doc?"

It was apparent that he really wanted to believe in ghosts. He though it was important for Americans to have them, too, like we weren't getting our fair share of what this infinite universe had to offer to both the living and the dead. Then I realized that what he seemed to be communicating was that life can be quite predictable most of the time. Everything here on Earth seemed to be understood or easily explained—with the possible exceptions of suffering a sudden and early death, such as during wartime. But now here was a chance for Numb-Nuts to believe in something new that's not easily understood, that takes faith and offers hope for something in life and death that we might not expect. So I said, "Yeah, Numb-Nuts, you're right. We should believe in them because ghosts are real."

* * * *

Charlie also made me realize that someone who died could still be an important part of life. I thought about how my dad must still think of his brother Mikie. I knew that Uncle Mikie had just graduated high school when my father started high school in 1921. All the Rabin kids attended Central High, located at that time on Cass and Forrest, but now my father had to catch the streetcar at the turnaround on Dexter and Collingwood to get to school. Uncle Mikie always made sure that Dad got on the streetcar, even though Dad had grown up in Detroit and, as a high school student, could easily take care of himself. But my father loved Mikie and didn't mind the attention. He enjoyed being with his older brother, and Mikie apparently enjoyed Dad's company as well.

Uncle Mikie had the personality and exceptional good looks in the family. He had black, wavy hair and an olive complexion, almost Sephardic looking. Mikie's quick wit and perpetual smile made him the kid that every other kid wanted to be. He gave dancing lessons in the house on Richton after school and had a waiting list a mile long. Dad loved hanging out and watching his brother, who was always the center of attention. Mikie was someone that everyone wanted to know and be like. "You're Mikie Rabin's kid brother, aren't you?" kids at school would say with obvious envy to my father. Mikie never made Dad leave the house when Mikie's friends were over, nor did he make Dad run errands and wait on his friends like some of the other kids' older brothers and sisters did.

Dad's sister, my Aunt Faye, got married before the family moved to Richton. And since Uncle Jack was always at the store and Bubbie Mollie often went there to help when it got busy, the house for much of the time belonged to Uncle Mikie and my dad. They were as close as two brothers, who weren't actually twins, could possibly be. When Mikie was killed, Dad was utterly devastated. In time, though, my father got on with his life. He wasn't a loner who was solely dependant on Mikie for friends and entertainment. Dad was smart and not bad looking either, as were all the Rabin kids. However, it was Mikie's ghost that for the most part kept Dad going after Mikie's murder. And I now know that it was also Mikie's ghost who was there to support my dad through his loss of Mikie, the depression and all the other rough times in his life.

* * * *

After talking with some of the ship's crew about Charlie, I realized that these guys, too, helped me grow into adulthood. I learned to accept the responsibility that other people respected and listened to my opinion. I knew that I had to think carefully about what I wanted people to hear because what I would say could severely impact their beliefs and emotional well-being.

My coming-of-age adventures weren't over by far, though. It would be a fellow sailor, Steve Schroeder, who would help me grow up intellectually. A trip to

Paris with Steve was an eye-opening adventure that would change the way I thought about the world forever.

The sailors on our ship, like I suspect was true of sailors everywhere else, didn't talk a lot about the Korean War. I know they thought about it, though, including the possibility that they too might be engaged in battle someday—a battle that might end in their death. The thought that ghosts existed, that there was something like a life after death, might provide some comfort. So it didn't totally surprise me that a young seaman like Numb-Nuts wanted very badly to know if ghosts were real. If ghosts were, in fact, real, then it just might give him hope that if his life on Earth ended soon, he may still be able to exist in some other form somewhere else. Thanks, Charlie!

Chapter 7

1953—Stephen Schroeder

He was a tall, well-built, nice-looking young man with a rugged face—but he had the eyes of a dreamer. He didn't look as young as most of us, who were in our late teens or early twenties, but he wasn't much older—maybe late twenties or at most early thirties. He was a deck ape who was more than able to keep up with the grubby-looking crew of younger swabbies, but his body language and facial expressions didn't look like those of a deck ape. A quiet man, he rarely participated in any activities with the rest of the crew, aside from doing his shipboard duties. In fact, most of the crew ignored him. With a permanent thin smile on his dark-complexioned, square-jawed face, he wore his Teutonic origins with quiet dignity and good-natured laughter. Some of the crew thought that Steve was a bit snobbish, but he was quite friendly once you did get to know him.

It seemed that he always had a notebook and pencil with him when he was off duty. He would sit around either staring into space or writing in his notebook, and then he would read over and edit what he had written. Even in a bar on liberty, we would see him writing in or reading from his notebook, usually oblivious to whatever might be happening around him. We could always walk up to him and greet him with a "Hi" or "Yo, Steve," and he would always respond with a gentle smile and a pleasant comment. Even sailors who didn't know him could approach him at some hangout and get the same smile and friendly treatment.

If they asked, "What you writing about?" he would always answer the same.

"Poetry," he would say with his warm smile. It was an unusual response for a sailor, but nobody every made fun of him or challenged his sexuality.

"What are you, some kind of fuckin' queer?" would not have been an unexpected comment from sailors in those days. Whether it was his large size or his gentle demeanor, something about him said that he was all right—just an EM with a hobby.

Stephen "Steve" Schroeder was the only son—he had a younger sister—of a wealthy Chicago businessman who wanted him to be a lawyer or have an MBA from some top-notch eastern school. When Steve graduated from high school in the early 1940s, he didn't wait around to be drafted—he enlisted in the navy instead. His parents were not thrilled, as they had wanted him to at least have started college. If he got two years of college in and was then drafted, he would have a better chance of going to OCS and becoming an officer. But Steve had no intention of going to college after he graduated high school. He never told his parents that he preferred to write poetry and short stories and read about the power of language and its ability to mold a societal ethos. After he made seaman first, he never tested for promotion to petty officer; he didn't want any military leadership responsibilities. Steve was more than content to serve in World War II on ships in the Pacific fleet, doing his patriotic duty—including combat duty—while reading and writing in his spare time.

When he mustered out of the navy in 1946, he used the GI bill to attend the University of Chicago, where he majored in English literature. Steve quickly got bored with most college course requirements, though, and took only those courses that moved him closer to his goal of becoming a writer. He took only English and American literature courses that were devoted to writing and poetry. Then at the end of his sophomore year, he wasn't allowed to register for the fall semester because he had failed to complete most of the basic requirements needed for continuing the program.

Not being readmitted to the University of Chicago was actually a difficult task, as the school was one of the most liberal in the country. Even at that time, Chicago allowed a great amount of freedom to students for selecting their program toward graduation. But, in addition to not completing enough required courses, Steve piled up many hours of incompletes for the classes he did sign up for and was on academic probation for his last three semesters because of his low grades. All that combined to get him kicked out of the University of Chicago.

Steve's family was concerned but supportive in his efforts to become a writer. Steve had written a number of poems, short stories, monographs, and even some scholarly papers on language and poetry, but nothing he wrote ever got published. His father continued to support him. However, he made it clear that if Steve didn't have a career or a job in two years, he would not receive any more financial support from home. "I do this for your own good," his father said. "Someday you will thank me for it."

*   *   *   *

For two years Steve continued to live near the university campus in an apartment that he shared with his girlfriend—she supported him with food and sex—where he did nothing but read and write. He decided that he needed to write "the great American novel" in order to get published, but he continued with his poetry writing as well. After two years, by the summer of 1950, Steve's father cut off his financial support, especially when he found out that Steve was living a "bohemian" lifestyle with a Jewish woman from the city.

"If you're as interested in supporting yourself as you say you are, then I'll get you a job with my company," his father said. "You can live at home until you feel financially capable of moving out and supporting yourself."

"I appreciate what you're trying to do for me, but I just feel that I have to keep at it—writing, writing, writing," Steve answered. "Thanks for the offer, and give my love to mom." So Steve stayed in his small apartment near the university, writing.

At the time his father made him the offer to come home, Steve was still waiting to find out whether his novel would be published. He had submitted an outline and about four chapters to a couple of Chicago publishing houses just about the time the Korean War broke out. Steve decided that if his novel was rejected, he would re-up in the navy so that he could continue with his dream of being a writer. Steve wasn't being rebellious or trying to prove something to his parents. They had been supportive of his efforts and truly loved him and wanted what they believed was best for him. However, Steve knew that his parents weren't able to fully understand his career goals or emotional needs.

When the rejection slips for his novel arrived in mid-July of 1950, Steve broke off his relation with his roommate—she was more than ready to move on—and reenlisted in the navy. After a short orientation for World War II returnees at Great Lakes, he was sent to duty aboard a destroyer tender in Norfolk, Virginia. Tenders rarely went out to sea, so it was like being on shore duty, even though you lived on the ship. In late 1951, Steve was reassigned to my future ship USS *Bock*, DDE 483. It was there that we met in early 1952.

* * * *

I first met Steve shortly after I came onboard but never got around to talking with him much until we went down to Key West, Florida. We were on our final shakedown cruise and refitting before heading up to Norfolk, Virginia, to join the sixth fleet. Steve was sitting on the fantail, which is where many of the off-duty sailors hung out when we were at sea. It was smoother riding back there, and there were lots of places to sit where you could just watch the ocean, in this case the Gulf Stream, and feel awestruck at being surrounded by aqua-green water and azure-blue sky. Some of the sailors actually tried to fish off the fantail, but unless the ship was steaming along slowly it didn't work very well. Most of the sailors were just bullshitting or commenting on the fishermen's luck, or lack of it. Or, like me, they just stared off into the sea and enjoyed the peace.

Steve was back there one day with his notebook and pencil, but I noticed that he too was doing more staring than writing. "What are you writing about today, Steve?" I asked. We all knew he wrote poems and stories, but no one knew much about them.

"I'm writing a poem about God's influence on Earth," Steve answered. "Have you ever heard of Alfred Korzybski—that's spelled 'k-o-r-z-y-b-s-k-i'—or his writings on general semantics?"

I didn't even know what the word "semantics" meant, let alone some theory of general semantics. And the name Korzybski was as alien to me as the spelling, which Steve did slowly and deliberately without making me feel like a stupid asshole. He then gave me a short but understandable lesson in what Korzybski was trying to accomplish.

"Alfred Korzybski was attempting in his teachings to help people better understand how the way an individual uses words could influence other people's thoughts and even their behavior," he explained.

"Like how?" I asked, truly interested in what Steve's work was all about.

He thought for a minute and then said, "A simple example would be like if I talked to you in a style that the Quakers used and said, 'How hath thou fared today?' You would have different feelings about me and you might even act differently towards me. That's a little oversimplified but you get the point."

In any event, it was Korzybski's work that was now influencing Steve's writings. Steve was taking a grand approach to it all by seeing if religion, or more specifically God, would have a different impact if the words used to teach religion were more modern. He added that the words used to discuss God should also be directed in ways that employed Korzybski's principles of general semantics.

"I'm composing a poem using two styles of English: the old biblical style—you know, with 'thee' and 'thou hast' words like in the example I gave you—and a more modern language style," Steve said. "I'm hoping to show through this poem that maybe people were missing something important or not really understanding God at all because they had been taught about God only in the old biblical style."

I was very much taken in by Steve's eloquent and understandable explanation. He didn't talk down to me, nor did he automatically assume that I would fully grasp what he was saying and be able to keep up with him in the conversation. He just acted like I had the innate intelligence to understand what he was about, and he wanted to share his work with me. I was honored by his willingness to talk with me at an adult level that he just assumed I would be comfortable with. He had no knowledge of my educational background and could care less if I was a college grad or a high school dropout. He knew, of course, that I was the corpsman. Sailors in general thought that corpsmen were more educated than most of them. I thought that maybe Steve just assumed that I had more formal education than I really did, but I found out later that that was not at all the case.

* * * *

About a week later, Steve asked me if I knew how to play chess, and if so, if I would like to play. I did know how to play; I had learned some basic strategies from a returning World War II vet who lived next door to me. I was eager to see how well I would do against Steve, so we got out a chess set and began to play.

Steve won white, so he got the opening move. After he opened with a traditional king's pawn, I was checkmated on the fourth move. Steve told me that it was called the "scholar's mate." He then began to teach me some other openings and how to protect against beginner's mistakes like the scholar's mate and the fool's mate. We began to play chess with some regularity; Steve would beat me almost all the time, unless he was distracted and made a foolish mistake. We also developed a friendship that was probably more beneficial to me than it was to him. I was hungry to learn about the things that Steve wanted to write about, and I wanted to read the kinds of books that he thought I should read.

Steve introduced me to the classics. I joined a classic book club where I bought a book every month by the likes of Aristotle, Plato, John Locke, and other philosopher-thinkers from Western culture. I also read some of Steve's poems, but I didn't understand a thing he was saying. I thought that maybe either I wasn't smart enough to understand them or just not educated enough. For example, he showed me a new poem that started out; "On a sunday morn in red house; i saw the sea shell's inner soul exposed."

Steve saw immediately that I wasn't getting his drift. When I finally admitted to him that I was lost, he explained what he was attempting to do in his poems.

I learned a lot about his poetry, which was mostly written in blank verse so it didn't rhyme. Like T. S. Eliot's work, they involved a lot of personal imagery, which no one would be familiar with, or know these images unless they knew Steve. I guess that somehow the images he used were supposed to transmit a universal truth that everyone should be able to understand. In any case, even when I thought I knew what Steve was trying to say, I really never got it or appreciated the message. I felt that his message was often convoluted and could have been said much simpler with greater meaning if he said what was on his mind. By using all the hyperbole and referring to unfamiliar imagery just left me with a disjointed message. But I was no poet and certainly not versed in literature, so I kept my opinions to myself and just commented in simple phrases like "Now that's interesting." I never said "Wow! What remarkable insight you've shown into the human condition," which is what I think Steve wanted to hear.

Even though Steve knew I wasn't getting his writings, he still listened to me and respected my opinion. He seemed to think that if I wasn't getting it, nobody would get it—not even the literary scholars. So Steve needed my feedback and tried to make his writings more in keeping with my comments and less in keeping with his idea of what poetry was supposed to do. In my opinion, Korzybski's work may not have had the most helpful influence on Steve's writing. I think Steve would have been better off conveying his message in his own way, using his own words and developing his own style.

During one of our conversations, I finally did tell him that I had dropped out of high school and took only art classes in my last year of school. He wasn't at all surprised and had actually guessed that that was the extent of my formal education. I asked, "Steve, do you think that because I quit school that maybe I'm not smart enough to go to college?"

He laughed and said, "Mike, I think you are a very intelligent monkey."

I wasn't quite sure what he meant by that, so I asked, "What the fuck is an 'intelligent monkey'?"

"Look, Mike, I know that you're not very well read and that you didn't finish school," he said. "I also know that somehow you picked up a lot of information somewhere along the way. And I'm really impressed with your vast awareness of almost everything—but you haven't demonstrated much depth in anything."

"So what does that all mean?" I asked.

"It means that you can bounce around like some monkey going from topic to topic, but you actually seem to know what you're talking about. I could have called you a dilettante, but that would have been an insult. An intelligent monkey was much more descriptive and not insulting." You can see why I could never understand his poetry, either.

It seems that it was my awareness of so many different subjects that impressed Steve; he was so narrowly focused, while I seemed to be all over the place. That was why he wanted my opinion on what he was writing. Furthermore, he said that there was no doubt that I could go to college and strongly encouraged me to do so. I guess I felt complimented but also a little surprised that he knew I hadn't finished high school.

"I'm just not sure I can make it in college," I said. "I hated all my schooling with the exception of corps school. I usually got so bored in the classroom. And I just faked it by memorizing everything." My voice must have reflected my own self doubts about my scholastic abilities.

"You just need to go to the right school and take the courses that interest you," Steve assured me. "College is so much different than high school."

Steve also pointed out that he had called me "intelligent" when I had asked if I was "smart" enough to go to school.

"What's the difference?" I asked.

"Intelligence is simply having knowledge, but being smart is the ability to apply one's intelligence to solve problems," he said. "Mike, I'm certain that once you're in the right educational setting, your intelligence will be honed and you'll be smart enough to apply that knowledge to many of life's practical and intellectual pursuits."

I didn't fully understand what he was saying about the difference between intelligent and smart, but I thought he was saying that I was still young and unsophisticated, but there was hope.

*   *   *   *

While our ship was in Key West we made some trips to various Caribbean ports. There was a small cadre of sailors aboard ship at that time that went on liberty with Steve Schroeder and me. Usually, we would end up at some bar drinking beer, talking, and joking about everything and anything. On occasion, we might get a little drunk and somewhat boisterous but never in the sense that you might think sailors normally do. We never, or rarely ever, got into fights or got thrown out of places. We also never had our liberty taken away by the shore patrol for being out of uniform or acting contrary to naval regulations. We were a fairly straight bunch of sailors.

I remember one night in San Juan, Puerto Rico, when four of us decided to go to an upscale luxury hotel. Like most luxury hotels in San Juan, the property was located on the waterfront and was rumored to have a luxurious and peaceful outside bar area called Jack's. So we decided to go there and do our usual drinking and talking. As we walked into Jack's, we saw a couple of young officers—JGs (lieutenants junior grade)—from our ship. One of them, Lieutenant JG Daniels, was Steve's shipboard officer and apparently knew about Steve's writing. They spotted us and greeted us cordially.

"How's your writing going?" Lieutenant Daniels asked Steve. "Have you written anything new?"

"Yes, my writing is truly showing progress, and yes, I do have something new," Steve said. "Would you like to see it now?"

Lieutenant Daniels seemed a little surprised. In a rather insincere manner, he said, "Well, if it's not too long, then yes, let me see it."

Steve assured him that it was short enough to read here and started to hand him his notebook, which was already opened to the new poem. Just when Daniels reached to take the notebook from him, Steve pulled it back and said, "Remember, you are not doing me a favor. I am doing you a favor." He then put the notebook in the lieutenant's hands. Daniels looked a bit stunned by that announcement but had no choice other than to take the notebook and read the poem.

I was also surprised by Steve's pronouncement. How grand that was—thinking that your artistic and intellectual efforts were of such a prize that someone would really be grateful for the chance to see or read them. I was a little embarrassed for Steve; as usual, his new poem was just as offbeat and hard to understand as the rest of his work. I thought that Daniels might have the balls to tell him that, but he didn't.

Daniels just smiled when he finished the poem and said, "Very good, Steve—very good." I knew Daniels was insincere, and I'm sure Steve knew it, too. Steve didn't seem bothered by Daniels's comment; for whatever reason, he was apparently unimpressed with the lieutenant. We went into the outdoor area of the bar and drank beer for as long as we could and still be able to get back to our ship on time. We talked of many things, but no one mentioned Lieutenant Daniels or

Steve's poem. I never asked Steve about his behavior that night, and I never heard him tell anyone else that he was doing them a favor by letting them read his work. I think Steve knew that Daniels was a phony, the type of officer who wanted the EMs to think he was just one of the guys, when in reality he was nothing more than an effete asshole. Steve's little performance was to let everyone know that. We were fortunate on the *Bock* to have very few officers like Daniels.

With Steve's prodding, I had taken and passed the GED—high school equivalency test—aboard ship. I also passed the two-year college equivalency test, which was called the 2CX. The 2CX made me eligible to go to OCS if I was interested and was recommended by my commanding officer. I also took some college courses in psychology and French through USAFI, a correspondence school run by the government. By early 1953, I decided to apply for college for the fall 1954 term at the University of Paris—the famous Sorbonne. I had heard that the Sorbonne was the place to go for artists, writers and anyone else interested in getting a solid European style of education. I wrote a letter to the Sorbonne asking for admission materials; stuck it in an envelope; addressed it to the University of Paris-Sorbonne, Paris, France; put a three-cent stamp on it; and mailed it from the ship's post office. Our exec, Mr. Miniard, later told me that it would never get there with only a regular first-class (not airmail) three-cent American postage stamp. Mr. Miniard's wife had attended the Sorbonne, so after he told me my stamp did not have enough postage to get my letter there, he good-naturedly asked, "Rabin, what makes you think they would even consider admitting you?"

In my favorite role as a wiseass, I told him, "I'm certain that the stamp was sufficient because I mailed the letter when we were out to sea; therefore, it needed no additional postage." I had absolutely no reason to believe that. "And I'm just as certain they will be thrilled to have an American like me studying with them in Paris," I added.

Minnie just smiled, nodded his head, and said in a teasing voice, "Yeah—bullshit!"

*   *   *   *

And so began my quest for a college education. A few months after that, in late March of 1953, our ship left the United States for a three-month cruise in Europe. When our ship entered the Mediterranean in May of 1953 and anchored off the coast of Nice, France, word went out asking whether anyone wanted to go to Paris. It seems that there was a three-day American Express tour available for servicemen for sixty-seven dollars that included three nights in a Paris hotel, transportation by train to Paris and return, and a meal on the train each way. Like most of my friends, I was flat broke from having spent all my money in Cannes the day before. But Steve and Gilbert "Gil" Laporte, another sonarman we went on liberty with, were planning to go and wanted me to come along. Steve had enough money to cover the tour, with a couple of bucks left over for food and drink. Unfortunately, Gil and I were totally busted, so we went around borrowing money—two dollars, five dollars, whatever we could get from anyone onboard ship who still had some money left. We carefully wrote down every loan to make sure that we kept track of all of them; if you ever reneged on a loan, you would never get another one from anyone else. We even took a motor launch out to the three other DDEs in our squadron that were anchored in our area. We borrowed money from whomever we could. Sixth fleet sailors were pretty good about lending money to sailors they didn't know well—even to sailors from other ships in the fleet.

We finally scraped up the money and went back to our ship, got our liberty passes, and took the launch into port where buses were waiting to take us to the train station. We had no money for meals or anything else, so I wired my father just before we left the ship. The telegram simply said "OFF TO PARIS STOP FLAT BROKE STOP SEND MONEY CARE OF AMERICAN EXPRESS PARIS STOP MIKE." My father saved that telegram for a long time, well after I was out of the navy. Gil had wired his folks for money when we were in Ireland and both of us were broke. Gil shared his money with me paying for our drinks, meals and bicycle rentals, and he felt that he couldn't ask his folks for more money so soon. As for Steve, he never asked his parents for money anymore.

We had dinner on the train that evening, and Steve bought a bottle of water to share for our included dinner—drinks were not included. It was Thursday evening when we arrived in Paris at our hotel: the Hotel Isly at 6 rue de l' Isly. It was an older elegant Victorian hotel that had survived World War II. We found out that the poor old hotel hadn't been modernized since World War I, so it was a bit tired. We were pleasantly surprised to find out that our tour package included a continental breakfast at the hotel, which meant coffee and French bread with butter and jellies. That was fine for us; after all, we were in Paris!

After we checked in we decided to do a little touring that night just to get oriented to the city. I had been trying to learn French from the course I took through USAFI and my remembrances of Rowle's accent. Moreover, I had pretty much memorized most of the major thoroughfares through Paris's city center, so I was the designated French translator and navigator. My first test was getting us back to our hotel by taxi. When we got into our first cab to go back to the hotel later that night I simply said, or thought I said, "Six rue de l' Isly." But because of my bad French accent, the cab driver took us to six rue de l'Elysee. After showing him the address neatly written out on a slip of paper, he repeated, "Ah! Six rue de l' Isly!" It was exactly like I had said it—or so I thought.

Back in our room—the three of us shared a room with two double beds—we planned our next day's activities. Before we had left on our Mediterranean cruise, I had received a reply from the Sorbonne regarding my request for admission to the university. It had come in an envelope made of thin, shiny brown paper and had contained a lot of forms, announcements, and other documents telling me what I needed to have in order to apply for admission. There were also a lot of French stamps on the envelope that I am sure were worth far more than the three cents I spent. After reading the admission requirements, I thought my GED and 2CX certificates more than qualified me to attend the Sorbonne's college of literature and science. However, one of the sections on requirements stated that I needed the equivalent of a French baccalaureate, and nobody aboard ship knew what that was. Some said it was a bachelor's degree, but Minnie seemed to think it was just a regular high school diploma, although he didn't think my GED certificate would be accepted as a regular high school diploma. So one of the things we had to do in Paris was find out about that baccalaureate requirement.

* * * *

Early Friday morning we went to the American Express office and picked up the twenty-five dollars my father had sent. We had hoped for more, but I hadn't been very specific about how much we needed, so we would have to make do with just the twenty-five. With Steve's seven dollars and change, we had over thirty-two dollars left for our three days in Paris; if we were frugal, it should be enough. After converting our money to francs, we took the metro over to the Saint-Michel station, and walked down rue des Écoles to the main entrance of the Sorbonne. The area we were in was called the Latin Quarter—a lively bar and restaurant entertainment center—and there were lots of young people and foreign visitors out walking. The old Romanesque buildings of the university were quite impressive and stood out from the typical four story walk-up apartment buildings and little shops that we saw on the street. The three of us, all in uniform, walked in and drew a few stares; we knew that we were being watched by the students with mild and not necessarily friendly interest. As we found our way to the admissions office, Steve pointed out, "You know those hostile looks could be because they think we're applying for admission. If we're admitted, we'd be taking up admission slots that could have been used by other French students."

I didn't think that my being admitted to the Sorbonne would be a problem to the other students, but Steve did make a good point. I had brought my admission papers with me, and we found someone in the admissions office who spoke English that we could easily understand. She carefully explained to me that the French baccalaureate exam was the equivalent of a United States two-year junior college degree. Apparently the French had two high school diplomas: one for anybody not going on to college and the other for college-bound students who successfully passed the baccalaureate exam. The clerk said that the average American high school diploma was like France's non-college-bound diploma; it wasn't sufficient, in general, for admission to the Sorbonne. She wasn't exactly sure what a GED test was, but she was quite certain that it didn't qualify as a baccalaureate exam, nor did my 2CX exam satisfy the requirement either. Finally, she gently pointed out that my French was not up to understanding the lectures or assigned readings by asking me, "Monsieur Rabin, do you think you can understand well enough your lectures and text books all in French?"

I had to admit, "Well my French learning is still progressing …, maybe by fall …, but you're right, my French is not good enough today."

To say I was disappointed was an understatement; my first attempt to go to college was a failure, and my naïve hope of studying in Paris with all the art and magnificent architecture around was shot down just like that.

We spent the rest of the day sightseeing around Paris and stopping to drink wine at sidewalk cafes along the way. We did get to the Louvre and actually saw the Mona Lisa in a gallery that was filled with other artwork; you could actually reach out and touch the painting in those days, although, of course, nobody did. We also saw the Winged Victory of Samothrace at the end of a long corridor. As we walked through the museum, I was getting more and more depressed that I wouldn't be able to study in Paris next fall surrounded by these marvelous works of art.

By nighttime we ended up on Pigalle—called "Pig Alley" by American servicemen then—in the Montmarte region of Paris. We were told that sailors like us—that is, not officers—would feel more at home around Montmarte than anywhere else on the Right Bank of Paris. Naturally, the Pigalle area was filled with bars, nightclubs, and prostitutes. Lots of American and French soldiers and sailors were walking the streets, looking to get laid by French hookers. We felt that we could get laid by prostitutes any time; that was the last thing we were interested in doing in Paris. However, we were getting pretty wasted on cheap wine and cheap snacks, especially the great-tasting, grilled ham and gruyere cheese *croque monsieurs* you could buy right off the streets.

* * * *

By around one a.m. we were wandering aimlessly around on a warm, clear spring night. We drifted over to the Rue St. Denis where the local farmers were bringing in their produce to sell in the market the next morning. Someone spotted us walking along—I guess we were a little wobbly—and immediately began yelling and screaming at us. As other farmers and their helpers saw us, they joined in the ranting. We didn't understand anything they said, but we knew they were angry with us. We were immediately aware of who their anger was directed at when we picked up on someone yelling, "American … go home!" We quickly left the area to avoid getting our asses kicked by the tough-looking farmers and instead walked along the well-lit Boulevard de Sebastopol.

As we approached the bridge over to the Ile de Cite, a young Frenchman, maybe thirty years old, approached us and spoke in angry but well-controlled English. "Why don't you go home? Why don't you leave? We have no hate for you, but we hate your government and don't want to see American soldiers on our streets."

I was shocked and hurt by that declaration: "We hate your government." I couldn't help but think about how Americans felt about the French just prior to and during World War II. The French wartime situation first entered my consciousness when the Depression ended in the United States and the war in Europe began to significantly impact our foreign policy. My father, who had recently turned thirty-five, and my Uncle Jack at forty were both exempt from the draft. The war changed many things, though; rationing affected the grocery store, and shortages affected the kinds of goods that my father could sell. However, the Rabin family didn't mind. They knew that the war was right and that Hitler and his policy of Jewish extermination and European enslavement had to be stopped. They would discuss it at family get-togethers during the holidays. "I can't wait till they kill that dirty bastard, that no-good sonovabitch," Uncle Jack would say about Hitler.

By the time the war turned in favor of the United States and the allies in 1944—the free French were considered our allies then—people were expressing hopeful optimism and discussing what life would be like after the war, and making plans for the future. When we went over to Uncle Jack's house to listen to a ball game one Sunday, he asked, "Did you see our new plans for the store? We'll have aisles for the customers to walk down with shopping baskets on wheels. It's the newest thing in grocery stores."

My father said, "I saw the same thing in that market on Dexter and Davison. Now they won't be able to take away your business."

However, much of the talk was still about the war. My sport's hero Hank Greenberg, the great Detroit Tiger, had enlisted, and I would have enlisted too if I had been old enough. In fact, I secretly hoped that the war would last until I was old enough to join, although I knew it was unlikely that the war would last five more years. Fortunately for the rest of the world, the war did end before I could get in. When I had my bar mitzvah in 1945, the war was rapidly coming to an end. I was in Durfee Junior High at the time and was relieved that after my bar mitzvah I would no longer have to go to Hebrew school. Life would be good again for the Rabins—especially for my Zadie Tzvi, who saw me, his favorite grandson, perform his bar mitzvah in front of the whole congregation. He also watched me give a speech that was written by my rabbi about the pen being mightier than the sword—a fitting post-World War II message.

I had learned many lessons from hearing about Bubbie Mollie's and Zadie Tzvi's Russian life and subsequent travels with their four children to America. One of the most important lessons I learned was to always believe that there was the opportunity for change for the better—no matter how daunting those changes might appear. I would see many newsreels and movies during the war of the captured French cities. They would show how sad and depressed the brave people in the French communities looked. I tried to picture the French singing "La Marseillaise" as we did in school, just waiting and hoping that help would come from the United States. It was time to pay Lafayette back and use our military strength to rid the French of the Nazis. We hoped that we could return the country to the France we all knew and loved. The behavior of the French I was seeing in Paris now surprised and saddened me.

Steve was philosophical about it all, speaking in a slightly slurred voice and pronouncing *s* like *sh*. "I think that market area around St. Denis is heavily communistic; it's in a communist area of Paris. I'm also quite certain that the communists are not excited with our 'police action' in Korea … fighting a communist government that was protected by, and a client state of, the communist Soviet Union."

We soon found a cab and went back to our hotel on rue de l'Isly around four in the morning, by way of rue de l'Elysee because my accent hadn't improved. By then I was more than depressed—first by my disappointment in not getting into the Sorbonne and then with the thought that if I did get in, nobody in Paris would want me there anyway. Steve was pretty much out of it by then, and although he was normally a quiet drunk, he did end the night on an interesting note. Just before he collapsed into bed, he stood up on his bed in his skivvies and loudly sang out "Amer-ican, go home!"—sort of to the tune of the Volga Boatman, "yo-oh, heave ho." It was quite humorous, but I still was feeling bad.

※　※　※　※

The next day, Saturday, we were hungover and started out late in the morning, almost missing our breakfast. We went over to the Eiffel Tower, second level only because we couldn't afford to go any higher, and planned on having a nice lunch there. However, the second-level restaurant was much more expensive than we thought it would be. We got a table near the window and ordered some of their cheapest wine, which still almost broke us, and just looked out over Paris under an overcast sky. The rest of day we continued to wander about, talking about the night before and wondering why the French hated us. We thought we had done so much for them in World War II, which was just a few years ago.

"Didn't we liberate Paris?" I asked. "And didn't they fall all over us when we marched in? Didn't de Gaulle tell us how grateful they were to have our friendship? So what the hell was all this hate about?"

We really didn't have a good answer, but Steve said, "I think the French think of us as arrogant and constantly shoving their faces into the fact that we liberated them. The French think we're too rich, we're too privileged, and we have too many material things that the French still don't have access to."

Gil joined in. "After all, it's 1953 and America is booming. We never saw any fuckin' combat on our soil. Our music, our shitty movies, our clothes, our cars, and anything American are being pushed all over the world as the stuff to have. And the French are still depressed financially." He paused briefly to light a cigarette, then added, "They're probably feeling guilty and shitty about once again in this century surrendering to the fuckin' Germans."

It seemed all very complicated and not worth endlessly worrying about it since we had no control over the world situation. But we did spend more time worrying about it. In fact, we spent the rest of the day and the rest of the night walking, drinking, and talking. At two or three on a very quiet Sunday morning, we used our last few francs to take a cab back to the hotel. As I waited for the driver to go to rue de l'Elysee and searched my pockets for the handwritten address, he pulled up to our hotel at six rue de l' Isly. Steve and Gil let out a loud cheer for me, and pointed out that after less than three days, I could now speak Parisian French—

what a coup! Later that night in bed, I still felt very sad and was in tears when I finally fell asleep just as dawn was breaking over the Parisian rooftops.

We left Paris on the early Sunday morning train, having had little sleep the night before and very little food. We hung around the train station a bit too long, so there were no seats left by the time we did get onboard. As a result, we had to stand in the aisle at the end of the coach all the way back to Nice. Whenever we tried to sit in the aisle, the conductor would yell at us and make us go back to the area around the head and either stand up or lean against the wall. When it came time for us to have our meal, we had no money left for anything to drink, not even a bottle of water. We asked for plain drinking water but were told that we shouldn't drink the water on the train. We were too thirsty to worry about it, so after much cajoling and some threats from Steve, the waiter finally brought us a pitcher of water—with a dead fly floating on top. We threw out the fly, drank the water with our included meal and then had to leave the dining car and go back to standing or leaning at the rear of the coach. We were quietly leaning on the wall and trying to sleep standing up when Steve slowly and in a deep voice started singing to that Volga Boatman's tune again: "Amer-ican, go home." Soon Gil and I were singing along with him. Our eyes were closed, but we were irreverently smiling.

* * * *

After going to Paris, I never again lied about my high school education. After I left the ship, I never got in contact with Steve again, although I thought about him a lot. I thought how he would continue to write and submit his work for publication, even though to the best of my knowledge he never got published while I knew him. I know he saved all his rejection slips, possibly to keep him motivated in pursuing his dream of being a writer.

Steve was instrumental in setting me on my pursuit of an education. Even though I was rejected by the Sorbonne, I knew that I would try to get into another school. And if need be, I would try many other schools. Sooner or later I would get in, just as I knew that sooner or later Steve would be published. Like so many of the other people I met in the navy, Steve was instrumental in my personal growth.

Steve also taught me how to conduct myself as an educated adult. He showed me that you need to feel pride in your artistic or intellectual pursuits. You can't let criticism deter you, but you can use it as a guide to greater accomplishments. Steve also taught me that one's efforts were valuable; you should expect your work to be appreciated by others. Finally, he made me think about the things I knew and how I could use that knowledge to examine other facets of life. And by critical thinking, maybe I could even come up with some general principles that would address the more complex social and political issues of our young lives. In other words, Steve taught me how to be smart.

When I think about real strides in my personal growth during my navy career, I definitely have to think about Steve Schroeder, but I also have to give a lot of credit to Homer Wilson, whom I would soon meet. Like no one else I had ever met before, Homer taught me that when life seemed to be totally unfair, and everything seemed to be stacked against you, you could still survive. Just like my grandparents survived Russia, Homer was surviving a prejudicial and uncaring world with humor, intelligence and the desire to flourish even in ways that may not be considered main-stream.

CHAPTER 8

1954—HOMER E. WILSON

"Campus swing man," he snickered, "tha's wha' you gonna be." Homer E. Wilson said that to me about a week or so before I was discharged. We had become close friends my last nine months in the navy. As it turned out, if I ever had to talk about one of the most memorable persons I had ever known, I would have to mention Homer E.

After coming off of sea duty, I was assigned to the Naval Air Station infirmary at Quonset Point, Rhode Island. The infirmary was like a small hospital with a dining room, wards (including a maternity ward), an operating room, an emergency room, a clinical lab, and other such facilities—all painted in hospital light green. I was there for a couple of weeks when I was put on night duty—that's thirty nights straight on duty from 8 p.m. to 8 a.m.—but my days were free to go on liberty or just hang out and sleep. I was the night assistant chief master at arms—an easy assignment for a second-class petty officer, but it was still night duty. The CMA (night chief master at arms) was Homer E. Wilson, a short, thin, fair-skinned African American career navy man.

Homer was one of the few first-class petty officers at the infirmary. My workstation was behind the front desk in the infirmary lobby, and I handled the routine, and sometimes not-so-routine, situations that might happen at night. The most common nighttime events were sailors involved in car accidents and sailors' wives having their babies. Homer was more or less responsible for the whole infirmary. Even though he also had a place to sit at the front desk, he usually just wandered around from the emergency room to the wards—wherever he felt like it. Homer was a lab tech and ran the infirmary's clinical lab. That's where he usually hung out at night—not the front desk—when he wasn't wandering the halls, doing stuff that none of us fully understood or were really concerned about, but he always looked busy and serious.

Homer would stop by the front desk for relatively brief periods of time, during which our conversations were short, formal, and at times almost hostile. One time we almost had a real fight when he tried to provoke me into saying things about him. "I heard you don't like me, and you've been saying some nasty shit about me. What you been saying?"

But I didn't take the bait. "I don't know what you heard, or who you heard it from, but it isn't true!" I responded.

"Oh yeah, well if I find out its true your ass is mine." He said, and Homer walked away grumbling. I was certain that he was going to put me on report for insubordination, and with less than a year left to serve, I was somewhat nervous about losing my stripes. I had no idea what he was talking about, but I knew none of it was true. Nothing ever happened, though, and Homer never mentioned it again. I had heard about Homer from some of the other corpsmen, but nobody really seemed to know him. They said that Homer was smart but difficult to get along with and that it was best to just avoid him.

On one of their daily visits, some Red Cross volunteers—called Gray Ladies because of their gray uniforms—left a chess set at the front desk for the patients to use. I never got around to moving it to the library, where hardly anybody ever went to, so the game stayed at the front desk. One night I had little to do, so I set up the chessboard and began to play by myself to kill time. Homer wandered by and saw the setup. He picked up a pawn and made a move, and then wandered off again. A short time later, he came back and saw that I had made a countermove. He quickly moved again but then hung around while I made my move. And that's how we started to play chess. We hardly spoke—it was a quiet night, which was the norm for that infirmary. We played for a few hours until by sheer luck I won. Homer didn't say anything after I said "mate," but he gently tipped his king over and walked away.

About an hour later he returned and for the first time since I was on night duty Homer took his seat at the front desk; he started talking to me. He asked me, "So where you from?"

"Detroit, Michigan," I said proudly.

"And did you learn to play chess in DEE-troit?" he asked emphasizing the first syllable in Detroit like many people not from the area.

"I learned to play from a neighbor guy who was a World War II vet," I said. "He taught all us neighborhood kids, or at least the ones who wanted to learn how to play. I think he told us that he learned the game in Europe from some Russian chess master." Homer nodded, as I paused to light a cigarette, and I said, "Actually, I really learned chess aboard ship from a seaman-poet by the name of Steve Schroeder."

Homer made a snide remark about "Steve the poet." Then he told me, "Well, I'm from Saint Louis, and I was the chess champion in my neighborhood. I taught the kids there how to play chess, but I'm no *master* and I can't rhyme a fuckin' thing." He told me that tonight was the first game he had lost in over ten years. From that night on, we became friendly—not friends yet, just friendly.

I was about the only person at the infirmary whom Homer talked with at any length. Sometimes we went bowling or to the gedunk stand on the base, either during the day or shortly before we had to go on night duty. Homer told me that as a second-class petty officer, I was entitled to a semiprivate, two-man room if any were available in the enlisted men's quarters. Because his former roommate had recently left Homer's two-man room, he asked me to be his roommate. There were not a lot of second-class or higher petty officers at the infirmary; most of the petty officers were third class and not entitled to a room. Also, all the other first-class corpsmen were sharing semiprivate rooms, and the few other second-class corpsmen that didn't have rooms weren't anxious to room with Homer. Some said it was because of his unfriendly attitude, but I suspect it was because he was black.

*   *   *   *

After our tour of night duty together, we got to know each other's "business" and started to become real friends, which meant that we trusted each other. My life was relatively simple. As I told Homer, "I grew up in a mostly Jewish neighborhood in Detroit. Quit school at seventeen, bummed around for a while, and then joined the navy when the Korean War started."

Homer's life was a lot more complex and involved a lifestyle that was not totally alien to me, but different to say the least. In fact, Homer was a different kind of friend—he was older, close to thirty, had almost eight years in the navy, and planned on being a career navy man.

"I joined up a year after high school. With the war over and with Truman in power, I thought the navy might soon be a good job choice," Homer said, meaning that he thought he could be something other than a ship's steward. "After boot camp, I went to corps school, which I knew had just opened up to us Negros. If I didn't go to corps school, I would have ended up a steward like everyone else, asking white officers, 'how do you like your coffee—like I like my women ... blond and sweet?'" His eyes twinkled as his face broke into a wide grin.

Homer's last remark was an old bromide going around that just about every African American steward claims to have said to some officer. Steward was essentially the only rating available to most African Americans prior to and during World War II, until Harry Truman fully integrated the military by executive order in 1948. Homer rose to first-class hospital corpsman after passing all the exams in the least time required—just under four years. However, he was never promoted to chief petty officer; even though he was sure he passed the exam for it when he was first eligible to test early in his second four-year tour. He knew that the reason he didn't get promoted to chief was because he was black. Given the era in which he was eligible, he was probably right.

"Did that piss you off?" I asked him about not getting promoted.

He wasn't bitter, at least so he said, "Nooo, little brother, I've been around the block, and I know who runs the fuckin' navy and that's the way things have always been and probably always will be." His emphasis on "No" sort of belied the fact that he wasn't bitter. At that time, a segregationist Southern U.S. culture dominated the military, in spite of Truman's executive order. Homer said, "Hey, I'm about makin my life the best possible it could be for me till I get my twenty in and retire."

Homer was married to a very "foxy" lady in Saint Louis named Ritah. Homer convinced Ritah that the navy sent her his entire paycheck, not just her dependant's allowance. So he asked her to send him some of it back for him to live on. Since Ritah had a job back in Saint Louis, she simply signed her check and sent it on to Homer. With his regular paycheck and Ritah's dependant allowance coming in every month, Homer was quite well-off by enlisted men's standards, but nobody else besides me knew about Homer's finances. He never flashed a lot of money around, nor did he buy a lot of stuff. All he privately owned was a small portable record player and a modest jazz record collection. Homer knew that I liked jazz, and we had many interesting conversations about musicians like Charlie Parker and Dizzy Gillespie. "Did you know that The Bird and Diz both smoked weed?" he once asked me. We talked about many of the great jazz artists of the forties and fifties, both black and white, who also smoked pot or did dope. The first record I ever bought on my own was Homer's recommendation: the 1953 album *Jazz at Oberlin* by Dave Brubeck. On Sundays when we didn't have any duty assignments, we would mix some ethyl alcohol—190 proof—with cokes. We'd sit around smoking a little weed, drinking our cokes, getting a buzz on and listening to jazz, including my new Brubeck album. I really enjoyed those days.

* * * *

In the late fall of 1953, I decided that I would need a car when I returned to civilian life. I flew home on a short leave and went with my dad to the Dexter Chevrolet dealer, where Dad had bought his very first car. I bought a brand-new 1954 Chevy with three hundred dollars down—money I had saved myself—and I agreed to pay thirty-five dollars a month for two years to pay it off. I bought insurance from the Auto Club because I needed it to finance the car. Dad helped out by paying the insurance premium for the first year. I drove it a day or so around Detroit to make sure it needed no major fix-ups, and then I drove it back to Rhode Island. Making the payments put a strain on my modest navy income, but it was worthwhile. To go anywhere from Quonset Point without a car required a lot of bus travel, and the bus routes were limited late at night. Having the car made it easier for me to stay out late.

As time passed, I learned more about Homer's "business" and became more involved in his personal affairs. Even though his nonmilitary lifestyle was different from mine, I had no problem adapting—a lesson learned quickly in the navy—and becoming part of the Providence, Rhode Island, scene. In particular, I became part of the small subculture of the African American neighborhood that Homer lived in when he was off the base. It seems that Homer had a separate and different private life going for him in Providence. In fact, all the time he was in the navy he would set up house in a civilian African American community near where he was stationed. Homer told me that he rarely socialized with other sailors, particularly white sailors—that is, until he met me.

Homer's life in Providence was mainly occupied by being the boyfriend of Ruby Letourneau (pronounced "le-TURN-er"). Ruby and her sisters were well-known in the Providence community where they lived. Most worked part-time as prostitutes and had their own pimps, but not Ruby; she had Homer. Ruby was a tall, nicely-built woman with silky smooth skin who I thought was very good looking. So were her sisters and most of her girlfriends. One friend named Pearly Mae was a slender, petite, "teasing tan" (Homer's description) nineteen-year-old girl. Homer also kept Ruby and her business associates and friends supplied with marijuana—"fifty cent a joint."

Homer was not Ruby's pimp—he was her man. He never hustled johns for her; on the contrary, Ruby hustled for him. Homer was her protector or at least acted in that role. Ruby gave him money because he told her that sailors didn't get paid very much. If she wanted him to come into town and take her out to clubs and supply her with dope and buy her meals and be her man, then she had to give him some money. In other words, like most of Homer's contacts, Ruby was just another business arrangement, but Ruby was deadly serious about Homer. Homer would have everyone believe that there was no emotional involvement between him and Ruby, but I knew better. When we would go into town and meet up with Ruby and her friends, Homer would never relax. He would look like he was drinking and doing some weed, but he would nurse a bottle of beer and hold back on the marijuana, which he called queen. He needed to be sober in case he had to do some business in town.

At first I was somewhat of a curiosity to Homer's Providence crowd. The first time I actually met them Homer made me wear my navy uniform. They knew that Homer was in the navy, and this way they wouldn't think it totally strange that he showed up with a white man. I didn't speak very much at first and answered questions with simple responses.

"You work up the hospital wid Homer?" Pearly Mae asked me with a wide smile and a sweet look on her street-hardened face.

"Uh-huh," I answered simply, avoiding eye contact keeping my face neutral, like what I did was some kind of secret not to be discussed further. After the first couple visits, I never wore my uniform again. I wore casual civilian clothes that I bought at a men's clothing store in Homer's neighborhood. In fact, Homer picked out most of the outfits. It gave me some credibility on the street to be dressed like the locals. I also began to speak like the African Americans in Providence, which was not unusual for me. I had already affected New England and Southern accents while stationed in Boston and Norfolk. I guess I talked in a fairly authentic Providence dialect for the neighborhood we ran in. In fact, Homer once told me, chuckling the entire time, that some people who had seen me with his crowd thought that I was a fair-skinned black man. I guess my close-cropped black, curly hair and olive complexion—just like my Uncle Mikie—helped in the ruse.

When Homer and I came into town, we would frequently double-date with Pearly Mae and Ruby. When I was dancing with Pearly Mae in the "black and tan" clubs and bars that we frequented, I rarely got stared at, which was a little unusual for that time period. After a few months, I could come into the neighborhood alone to meet up with Homer at no determined time or place—I just had to find him. I would walk into one of the bars where Homer did his work, toothpick hanging out of the corner of my mouth just like Homer. I would walk up to someone I recognized through Homer or Ruby or Pearly Mae and ask, "You see my people?" I would usually be told whether Homer or Ruby had been there and where they might be now, and so I would simply go off and find them.

Homer's trips into town were always more business than pleasure. He would either try to sell dope, set up business arrangements with some other people he knew, or meet with Ruby and get some money from her. Doing business was an obsession with him. He was constantly thinking of ways to make money but always from a counterculture market that few white people really knew or understood. For example, Homer told me that when he was stationed in Brooklyn he had a girlfriend, just like Ruby, who he stayed with up in Harlem. When he wanted to do some business on Sunday mornings, he would get into his uniform and go out early, unshaven and looking a little wasted. He would mess up his jumper a little like he had been sleeping in it and then head into Midtown Manhattan. There he would walk around until he spotted a mark that he would approach and say, "Hey, fella, I was up in Harlem last night and got rolled. Can you help me get back to my ship?" After he made around fifty bucks—a lot of money in 1953—he would come home feeling that his time was well spent; he hadn't wasted Sunday morning not doing business. Homer's girlfriend never knew what he did in town—again, that was his business—she only knew he went in to work. Homer told me that was the easiest money he had ever made. White people were more than willing to believe that a poor, skinny, inexperienced-looking black sailor with a gentle Saint Louis accent could easily get rolled in Harlem.

* * * *

Selling marijuana was one of Homer's favorite ways to make money. Occasionally he would score some in Providence, but more often than not he would get it from other sailors on the base. Homer knew most of the African American sailors stationed on the base, and being a corpsman, he could do them some worthwhile favors. One way of getting favors owed was to perform various lab tests for the sailors or their girlfriends that they didn't want to make public. There was one particular contact of Homer's that we called Cookie—not only was his last name Cook, he was a navy cook as well. Cookie got Homer a lot of dope from New

York. He would make weekend trips to the city whenever he was able to and bring back all kinds of stuff—grass, heroin (which he called "horse" or "king" back then), and some pills that we never even heard of. Cookie would sell most of it to other sailors to support his own heroin habit; he was a heroin junkie. He would come into our room, shoot up his dope and then nod off. Homer, in turn, sold or traded dope with Cookie for needles and eyedroppers, which were preferred over syringes because they worked easier than a syringe when you had only one hand. Neither Homer nor I ever used heroin, but we wouldn't let any of the suppliers or users know that. Most of Homer's contacts believed that Homer would shoot up once in a while, which made him more trustworthy in their eyes.

Cookie wasn't sure about me and was always confused as to what I was—black or white or somewhere in between. I treated him harshly and kept telling him "get your shit together my man, or else you gonna end up either in jail or dead." He didn't like that, and if he knew I was just another white sailor, I think he would have tried to hurt me. In any case, I realized that I was engaging in some very dangerous behavior by riding Cookie like that. Homer warned me on a number of occasions that I was asking to get myself hurt if not actually killed.

When Homer had a stash of marijuana, we would roll them into joints on the weekend and sell them later in town. Homer didn't sell dope on the base; he did all his dope-selling business in civilian clothes in Providence. When Cookie didn't come through with some marijuana, Homer would improvise by mixing what weed he might still have left with a variety of other things, including Bull Durham tobacco, which was cheap and came with a pack of cigarette papers. One time when Cookie didn't deliver, I found Homer on the base picking some leafy weeds from a grassy area near the runways. I didn't ask him why he was pulling weeds; I just joined in with him. He told me exactly which weeds to pull. We went back to the lab, where Homer took the weeds and carefully dried and browned them in the hot dry-air sterilizer. After letting them dry out for a few hours more, he crushed them into little pieces, mixed in some left over dope and cigarette tobacco, and rolled them into joints.

We went into town that night and were drinking in Fillipe's bar when someone came up to Homer and started the standard conversation. "Hey, baby, wa's happenin'?"

"Evrathin' happenin', my man," Homer said, and off the two of them went to the men's room. Later when Homer came back he said to me, "Le's get out of here. I just sold that dude six joints of that weed and shit for four dollars, so it best we leave now." He went on to tell me that he had told the dude, "Now this shit was new stuff. It comes from overseas and is posed to be very, very strong; tha's why it gonna cost you a little more; you okay with that?"

He shared one joint with him so the dude could try it out, and Homer watched as the dude got high. "Man, tha's some good shit alright," the buyer said. Homer figured that sooner or later the dude he sold the homemade mix to or one of the dude's friends would catch on and come looking for him.

*   *   *   *

I already mentioned that Homer was a skinny little guy, but it was amazing how many people were physically afraid of him. Homer had a little push-button pocketknife that he carried around. He bought me one, too—I think they were about seventy-five cents then. He modified the knife for me by taking out the spring that popped the blade open, but he left the blade-locking mechanism in place. When I took the knife out and pushed the release, the blade didn't spring out feebly as it would normally; it just sat there, ready to be opened and locked. Homer then taught me to flick my wrist, and the blade—all four inches of it—would fly out and make a solid click when it locked into place. As formidable as it sounds, the knife would never hold up under close scrutiny. In fact, it could put you at risk if you actually tried to use it in a confrontation. But use them we did—although on very rare occasions and for bluffing purposes only. Homer and I would flip them open only if the time called for it and we knew, or at least thought we knew, that we could get away with it. We never actually stuck anyone, but it was great bravado and fortunately for us—me as a white man, in particular—nobody ever called our bluff.

I can remember one time that Homer, Ruby, Pearly Mae, and me went to a little diner located on a bridge over a canal near downtown Providence. It was about 4:30 in the morning, and the diner was usually crowded then with people wanting some coffee and maybe a sandwich or sweet roll after being out all night partying. Folks from the neighborhood also socialized there without the distractions of music, booze, and dope. People would talk and eat at the counter or even while they were standing-up waiting for a seat—wherever they could find some room in the little space that's where they gathered. That night we squeezed through the crowd until halfway down the counter Homer stopped and turned around. He then very publicly and loudly walked back a couple of steps and stomped on this guy's foot about as hard as you can imagine. Now the guy he stomped on was big—well over six feet tall and probably more than 250 pounds—by far the biggest and meanest-looking guy in the place. The diner went silent. Then the big guy, with a look in his squinty eyes that scared me asked, "Why you stompin' my foot?" Homer calmly told the big guy, "Hey brother, you stepped on my foot when we was passen by—I just did you like you did me."

"Why, you little flea! You skinny little muthafuka, I'm gonna pick you up and throw your muthafuken ass in the canal!" The big man said that in a deep, throaty voice and the meanness in his eyes was like nothing I'd ever seen before.

The diner was small enough that everyone could see what was going on, and they waited in shock to see what would happen. Nobody uttered a word except for the pleading of Ruby and Pearly Mae. "Homer, le's get out 'a here!" Ruby cried. "Le's leave—you know who that is."

Homer backed up a little, pulled out his little blade, and with much fanfare flipped it open—*CLICK!* Holding it low in his right hand, he said, "You a dirty lie, muthafuka—come on."

Now I knew Homer well enough to know that he had a good reason to do this and that nothing would probably come of it. So I stood behind him and softly said, "I'm right behind you, little brother. I'll back you up till your belly caves in."

Well the big guy kept on yelling and threatening while the four of us backed slowly out of the place through the back doorway. The poor girls were very scared but were more than impressed by Homer's bravery and my standing by him (which today I realize was pretty stupid). They gushed all over us the entire way back to Ruby's place. Later, when Homer and I were driving back to Quonset Point, I asked, "What was all that shit in the diner about? Why did you take on that big son-of-a-bitch?"

Homer told me, "That big fucker is a well-known, strong-arm bully; I don't know his name but people round here call him Mac. He even killed someone with his two bare hands many years back, but he only got sent away for manslaughter, not murder like it should have been. He'd got out some time ago but was sent back to prison for doin another felony crime. I heard earlier that Mac was being released today, and we might be runnin in to him around the block. I knew that if Mac get busted again, he would be called a habitual criminal and probably would get a life sentence, so I figured Mac the thug knew that, too."

So Homer took a chance to make himself look like a hero and pulled off that crazy stunt. In a short time, word was all over the street that Homer had started a run-in with Mac the "murderer" and had just stared him down. That was a lot of cachet for Homer in the neighborhood, and it just added to the respect that folks had for him. It also didn't hurt my reputation in the neighborhood either, making it easier for me to walk around alone without being bothered by anyone. What I didn't realize at the time is that it also made me marked for some possible serious payback in the future.

* * * *

Dealing with druggies can be a dangerous venture, and several times we came close to getting into real trouble with the police. One of those times occurred when we were driving around the neighborhood and Homer spotted someone he knew who had recently been released from prison on drug charges. Homer thought he might be able to find out whether there was any stuff for sale in the area, so we stopped and picked him up. He was a very nervous man, and as it turned out, he was looking to score himself. He thought that Homer might be able to get him some dope—either marijuana or heroin. Homer quickly realized that this wasn't a good idea, so he asked the guy, "Hey man, where you wanna be dropped cause we outa here?"

I was driving and the junkie told me to take the next right turn. He either forgot the neighborhood or they had changed it after he went to prison, because turning right set me going down the wrong way on a one-way street. In addition, in the middle of the street was a police car with its lights flashing, and next to the police car was a dead man lying in the street. Well, the nervous dude was literally beside himself—jumping up and down, and screaming, "Hey man, hey man turn around! Turn the fuckin' car around—we gotta get outa here, I mean now!"

He was trying to open the door so he could jump out, and Homer kept saying, "Be cool, jus be cool ..." while I continued slowly down the street and then turned off at the first chance I got. All the time we were going down the street, one of the police officers just stared at us, apparently not sure what to do since his priorities were obviously somewhere else at the time. As soon as I turned off the one-way street and was certain that we were out of sight, I stopped the car and the junkie jumped out and ran.

In the meantime, I saw Homer breathe a sigh of relief. It turns out that Homer had scored earlier and had a shitload of stuff on him. The last thing we needed was for the police to stop us with a known dope head in the car and Homer with all his stuff on him. We certainly would have been in some serious trouble. Actually, I knew that the junkie and Homer would have been in more trouble simply because they were black. I knew justice wasn't evenly played out. As Homer told me, the worst that would have happened to me once I showed my navy ID was that I would get a stiff lecture for trying to buy marijuana from "those people" in "that neighborhood." It was Homer who always took the risks, and somehow or other he was lucky enough and smart enough to get away with a lot of very risky behavior.

* * * *

My last three months at Quonset Point—which, incidentally, were my last three months in the navy—were spent on night duty. This allowed me to put away some money for college and make my car payments. I didn't make it into town very often, spending most of my spare time either in the library visiting with Ann Baxter, the infirmary's librarian, or simply reading. I saw Homer only when we were in our room at the same time, which was mostly on Sunday mornings. I never saw Pearly Mae again, but I'm sure she wasn't surprised. We were just friends enjoying each other's company once in a while; we both knew we would never be tight like Homer and Ruby. I had only one other occasion to go into Providence at night those last three months, and it was quite a show.

I got a call around two in the morning in the middle of the week from Providence General. "Can I please speak to Mike Rabin, the assistant chief master at arms?" the ER clerk on the other end of the line asked. The clerk told me, "We have a first-class petty officer by the name of Homer E. Wilson here; he was brought in over an hour ago suffering from multiple cuts and stab wounds over his face, chest, and arms. He's been treated by the emergency room staff and has requested transportation back to Quonset Point. He told me that you, as the assistant chief master at arms, could arrange that. Is that right? Can you arrange for his transport?"

Knowing Homer I knew it wasn't life threatening because that would not be the message I would have received from him, so without missing a beat, I told the clerk, "Yes, that's correct. I'll arrange transport and have a vehicle there to pick up Petty Officer Wilson within an hour." I then followed through on the inquiry by asking, "Has there been a police report filed?"

The clerk said, "Wilson told me that you would also handle that—is that right?"

I naturally agreed and with some authority said, "Yes, that's the correct procedure to follow. Our SPs will file the report once Wilson is back on base."

It's a good thing I knew how Homer thought; I gave out all the right answers without any hesitation, or I'm sure Homer could have ended up in jail.

I knew that Ruby carried a small, sharp nail file that she used for protection. She didn't want to carry a knife, thinking that if she used it, it would in all likelihood be her who would get into trouble. But a nail file was not considered a weapon. If Ruby used it on someone, it could always be construed as self-defense and certainly not a premeditated action. When the ER clerk at Providence General told me that Homer had a number of cuts and stab wounds, I knew immediately it was Ruby. I had a navy license for driving ambulances, so I found the CMA and told him, "Chief, Homer has been hurt in Providence—it wasn't life threatening—but he needed to be picked up and brought back to the base. It's a quiet night, so why don't I just go into town and bring Homer back rather than wake up the duty ambulance driver. What do you think?"

The CMA said, "Yeah, sure Rabin, why don't you just go and get him. I'll cover for the both of us." So off to town I went in one of our elegant, hearse like 1950s Cadillac ambulances to get Homer.

When I got there, Homer was waiting for me with all kinds of little bandages and Merthiolate splotches on his face and arms—and probably on other parts of his body that I couldn't see. He didn't say anything but had a silly grin on his face and just started to chuckle.

I couldn't resist saying, "Well, Mr. Lion, you didn't fare so well. Your face is all fucked up, and you look like hell." That was a line from "The Signifyin' Monkey," an African American folk poem that Homer had taught me after Cookie accused me of always "signifyin'." In other words, I would ride Cookie almost to the point of him wanting to hit me and then backing off.

"Ruby tore me up somethin' fierce," Homer said.

"Why did she cut you?" I asked.

All he would tell me was that she was a very jealous lady and that he had gotten caught in some kind of a lie. I never found out any more about it. A week or two later I did find out that he and Ruby were tight again and everything was business as usual.

* * * *

In the navy you change duty stations quite often, and you make some very fast friends who you are sure you will keep in touch with for the rest of your life. At first, like right after boot camp, you cry when you get your new duty assignment and you swear to write and stay in touch with the guys you became brothers with. But after a few years, you become a lot more inured to the process and usually just shake hands and say, "See ya around!" With Homer it was different. He had a pat little speech that I heard him use many times when people would leave, but he never said it directly to anyone's face. I heard it so many times that I learned it by heart. "If you see me comin' down your side of the street, don't cross over—I will. Don't wave at me, and I won't wave at you. Don't look back, 'cause I won't be lookin' back." We both said that little ditty together, with smiles on our faces and tears in our eyes.

I've thought of Homer many times since I last saw him the day I left the navy. He taught me so many things about surviving and living in an unjust world, how someone could try and isolate himself so that nothing—neither love, nor friendship, nor death—would bother him, but it really didn't work. I also realized how lucky I was—a Jewish kid from Detroit—to have the opportunity to stick my little toe into a small, obscure slice of African American culture and learn to appreciate its color, its sadness, its unfairness, and even its joy.

In all the time Homer and I spent together, including the close calls we had with authorities and civilians, almost getting injured or killed, Homer was always smiling right after it was over. Life was good! He knew that he "rounded the corners on my square ass," as he was wont to tell me many times. He also knew that I wasn't going to be a "swing man"—local parlance for a dope pusher—when I went to college. Through all his business dealings and what white folks might think of as amoral, or at worst immoral, behavior there was a very basic survival plan. Homer's goal was to one day retire with Ritah in Saint Louis and lead a quiet, comfortable, prejudice-free life—just listening to some sounds on the box while drinking a little ninety-five and coke.

CHAPTER 9

1954—ANN BAXTER

Night duty at the Quonset Point infirmary had its advantages, besides allowing me to save money for school. I had the run of the infirmary and could go just about anywhere I wanted. It was during those last three months that I really discovered the library: a small room with a lot of gray books neatly shelved in stacks and divided into categories like mystery, nonfiction, and poetry. I wasn't much of a reader; I preferred to draw—or I should say copy pictures out of storybooks and comics. But, I had developed a taste for poetry from my discussions with Steve Schroeder, so I liked skimming through the poetry books.

One night while I was looking through the poetry section I found *Modern American Poetry: A Critical Anthology*. Edited by a Louis Untermeyer, the book featured collections of poems by the likes of Walt Whitman, E. E. Cummings, T. S. Eliot—I had thought Eliot was an English poet!—and many more classic American poets. The book also included commentaries on the poets' lives and works. It was last revised in 1942, which made it twelve years old, but it was in excellent condition. I could see from the sign-out card that it had been checked out only once before on June 7, 1952, almost two years ago; obviously not a popular book among sailors. Inside the front cover was a date stamp of 1949. Over the stamp someone had written the word "gift." So the book had joined the navy in 1949, about a year before I joined, and was checked out only once in all that time—how sad, I thought. Here someone had made a gift of this marvelous book of poetry, and no one seemed to care—sad, yes, but not surprising. I started reading some of the poems and got hooked. After reading the book for about an hour, I took it with me without checking it out. Whenever I had the opportunity, I would read from that book of poems, trying to understand what the poets were saying and what it might mean to me. Most of these poems rhymed, and unlike Steve Schroeder's poems, I could understand them.

*   *   *   *

On rainy days or days I couldn't sleep, I would go to the library and skim over other books—poetry, and sometimes science fiction—or just wander around looking at the collection. Hardly anyone else came to the library, but it had a full-time civilian librarian anyway. Ann Baxter, it said on her desk nameplate, was a tall, gangly, plain-looking women in what I guessed were her late twenties or early thirties. She wore huge glasses that looked like two bicycle tires. All I could think of was that she must have been the model for Dorothy Parker's poetic quip, "Men seldom make passes at girls who wear glasses."

Ann noticed I always migrated to the poetry and science fiction sections. I also had a feeling that she knew I took the poetry anthology book and never returned it, but she never called me on it. Our first conversation started one day when I casually asked, "Are you related to Anne Baxter, the movie star?" How lame was that conversation starter?

She smiled warmly and said, "No, but people often ask me that question." She pointed out that the movie star's name was Anne Baxter while she was simply Ann—no *e* on the end. "Surprisingly," she said, "we're both originally from Indiana."

She didn't look anything like the movie star, but I would never have told her that. "So—I've noticed you looking at the poetry and science fiction books," she continued while she did some paper work on her desk. "What books interest you?"

I told her that I had no particularly singular interest; I was just looking for something to do to pass time while I was on night duty. "I'm a short-timer now and I'm planning on going on to college when I get out," I explained. "The navy granted me a three-month early discharge to go to school, so I applied for early discharge and it was approved. I'll be getting out in July."

"Well, that's good news," she said with her huge glasses seeming to put exclamation points every time she talked. She stopped doing her work and looked up from her desk saying, "You said that you don't have any one type of book that interest you; right? Do you ever read novels?"

"Not really. I guess my idea of a novel is *My Gun Is Quick*. That was written by Mickey Spillane, but you knew that, right? I heard that's just pulp trash." I said that a little sheepishly because I was embarrassed that I couldn't name one real novel I could talk about.

"You know, I think I have a book that you would like." I followed her over to the stacks where she pulled off a book and handed it to me saying, "I think you might enjoy this. It's written by a relatively new author whose name is Ross Lockridge; the book's called *Raintree County*. It came out in 1948, and it was quite controversial at that time."

Well, needless to say, I really enjoyed it. The book took place during the civil war and the main character was a Job-like person in that horrible things kept happening to him, yet it never got him down. I had never read anything like it and was impressed by the different philosophies and opinions that the key characters expressed. I identified strongly with the misanthropic Jerusalem Webster Stiles, the guy who was always seeing the worst in everything and everybody. I guess you would call him the foil character or antihero; he was the opposite of Shawnessy. When I told Ann that I liked the book and identified with Stiles, she was upset because she was hoping that I would identify with the hero, Shawnessy. He was the guy who, no matter what happened to him still saw hope and beauty, not the despair and mistrust of "Perfesser" Stiles.

I could tell that Ann thoroughly enjoyed helping me understand the power of books. Without a lot of fussing and preaching, she led me through the library and showed me where all kinds of things could be learned or simply enjoyed. She knew I hadn't read a lot but didn't act snobbish about it and was genuinely impressed that I had read several of the classics—Plato, Homer, and the like—while on sea duty. She also was delighted when I told her that I had made notes in the margins like college students did—or at least that's what I was told they did.

I almost got the feeling that Ann didn't want to lose me as a customer since I was one of the few people at the time—in fact, maybe the only person—who was using the library and her services on a regular basis. I also think she enjoyed showing me what to read and what I should look for in the book. Ann always had a big smile for me that seemed to match her big eyes; I couldn't help but also smile broadly each time we met. When I came to the library to return books we would talk about them and then she would recommend a new book or two, and off I would go until a few days later, sometimes longer. When I returned them Ann acted like she couldn't wait to get my opinions and thoughts about the authors and their books. She would ask me all sorts of questions, like, "So what did you think of Wylie? How do you think he compares to Wells?" she asked once.

I answered, "I don't know ... I think Wells reads like a book, but Wylie reads like a magazine. Does that make sense? Both were fun to read."

After a little discussion about the authors' styles and commonalities and her sharing some personal insights she would recommend some other books for me to read. Her recommendation would be based on our conversation and her feelings about the subject. I might add that there was little doubt that religion played a big part in her life, and I think she wanted religion to play a part in my life as well. It was almost like she knew what I was going to say about the authors and she had a new reading list ready and waiting for me.

Besides introducing me to the two greatest sci-fi writers of the times—Robert Heinlein and Isaac Asimov—she had me read Edward Bellamy's *Looking Backward*, an 1888 book that many consider the first American sci-fi novel. The book described what Bellamy thought the United States might look like today, and seeing how different his vision of the future was compared to how it really turned out taught me a powerful lesson: authors who predict the future are not always accurate. Realizing that sci-fi authors didn't necessarily know what the future held was a simple but lasting lesson. Even authors with great imaginations and a good scientific understanding of technology, such as H. G. Wells, couldn't accurately depict or predict the future.

In addition to science fiction, Ann also got me interested in the modern thinkers of the day. The names may mean little today, but in the early 1950s, they were authors who had started something of a revolution in social awareness. Nathanael West's *The Day of the Locust* was his commentary on the decadent life style of Hollywood and Los Angeles. His *Miss Lonelyhearts* was a superb commentary on the struggling lives of people who were alone even in a crowd. Both of those books were published in the thirties and were on all freethinkers' lists of must-read books. When I learned that Nathanael West had a Russian-Jewish background similar to mine—he even changed his name from Nathan Weinstein—I thought I had found my literary hero. I was deeply disturbed when I found out that he had been killed in a car wreck in Los Angeles in the late 1940s.

Philip Wylie's *Generation of Vipers* bordered on science fiction like many of Wylie's other books. But he used the sci-fi genre not to discuss technology, but only to point out social issues (like women's equality) in a short story format. There were other authors and books that I had read prior to coming to Quonset Point that influenced my thinking and how I looked at the world. But my intellectual maturation that actually started aboard ship with Steve Schroeder was now being polished by my new guide, Ann Baxter.

* * * *

Through all the recommendations and post-reading discussions, Ann and I had kept a close and warm friendship. She was the big sister I didn't have; she really cared about what I thought and what I felt and wanted to make sure I was prepared for college. She knew that even though I had my GED and had read some classical works, my academic preparation was spotty at best. I'm sure she felt like she was molding me into something she could be proud of. She continued to push me toward the hopeful side of the world and away from the cynical pessimism that drove a lot of my behavior and earlier actions. But more importantly, she convinced me that I should consider a writing career. I might also have a story to tell—maybe one that would influence other young people to always keep on questioning the people who were running the world. And the most important thing they can do for themselves is to never lose hope that they will achieve more than they could ever imagine.

As I continued to read and grow under Ann's guidance, I often thought about the other close friends I made in the navy—friends like Rowle Pelletier, Billy Pierce, and my latest buddy here at Quonset Point, Homer Wilson. I wondered how and what my earlier pals were doing. I also wondered about the other people who had influenced me—Major Dumont, Steve Schroeder, Sister Marie Therese, Rosie Domokos. I reflected on the whereabouts of guys like Bobby Johnson and his fellow deck apes—even the jokers like Numb-Nuts. But more often than not, when I would start to reflect on those guys I would come back to wondering about old Black Tooth.

Every now and again, I would run across someone who would tell me about one or another of the many folks I met and simply forgot about. For instance, shortly after I came to Quonset Point in the fall of 1953, I went up to Brockton and spent a Sunday with my old friend, and now civilian, Billy Pierce. He met a corpsman that I went to corps school with who knew and remembered me, Mike Rabin, and remembered me in a positive way. Maybe they didn't remember me as a hero like the major, but they still were good enough memories to give me hope for the future—hope that I might turn out to be someone my family would one day proudly say of, "he's one of ours."

* * * *

After I was discharged and admitted to the University of Michigan in the fall of 1954, I placed out of freshman English, mostly because of the impromptu essay I had written about Alfred Korzybski—how about that, Steve? I took advanced English courses, Shakespeare, English poetry, and writing. Though I didn't become a writer, I did began to realize the dream that Ann and some of my earlier mentors—especially my grandparents—had in mind for me.

My grandparents Tzvi and Mollie Rabin had come from Russia with little formal education and even fewer possessions. They brought four kids to a new country, along with their set of values: the Jewish need to be educated, and the Russian toughness to survive. They came with hope that there would be no more anti-Semitism and that their kids could learn and be safe in their home. They were blessed with six grandchildren and devastated by the senseless loss of their son, Mikie. Zadie Tzvi loved all his grandchildren, but there was no doubt that I was his favorite. It was me, almost as soon as I started Hebrew school after kindergarten that went to shul with him. And it was me that Zadie Tzvi, unknown to my parents, enrolled in the yeshiva so that I could become a rabbi. Even though I got my parents to quickly take me out of the Hebrew parochial school and put me back into the public school system, my Zadie Tzvi never loved me any less for not going on to become a rabbi.

Someone once said that you should be careful what you wish for because you just might get it. I don't think that applied to my zadie; I think all Tzvi Rabin ever wished for, he almost got. I think all he wanted, "God willing," (as he said frequently) was for his children and grandchildren to live in a world at peace. He wanted his family to be educated and free from hate and discrimination. Well, all of that didn't quite happen. Even so, enough of it did from time to time to give Zadie Tzvi hope that he might indeed get what he was wishing for—hope for a future that had more promise than I could ever imagine. "Rub up, Uncle Bill, just rub up."

Epilogue

▼

WHITECAPS

It was on a Wednesday in early June. I had just gotten off of night duty and was starting my morning routine. That consisted of breakfast, then going out with a small group of night corpsmen to play twenty-seven holes of golf on the base's tiny par three, nine-hole golf course. Usually after golf we would go back to our quarters, shower and shave, and then try to sleep some before getting ready for another night of staying awake. But today was just too nice to waste trying to sleep. My head was full of thoughts about my college plans. All I could think about was that next month I would be discharged, and then soon after that I would be in college. I had no idea what I would major in. I still hadn't heard whether I was accepted for fall admission at Michigan. I still hadn't decided whether I should also apply to Wayne University in Detroit. But this morning, all I was thinking about was James Russell Lowell's poem that starts out, "And what is so rare as a day in June?" It was a rare day, indeed. The sun was bright, the sky was clear and blue, and soft, late spring breezes were blowing in from the east off of Narragansett Bay.

I changed quickly without showering or shaving, got in my car, and drove off the base to a little secluded beach area that some of us used for digging up and steaming quahogs. It was well before noon. The breeze was cooler here, and not another soul was around. The easterlies had blown up small whitecaps on the bay, and the water was like the typical black and green waters of the Atlantic. I found a nice spot to sit down and reflect on my life—present and future. I recalled a few more lines of Lowell's poem:

> Joy comes, grief goes, we know not how;
> Everything is happy now,
> Everything is upward striving;

Today seemed to be one of those extraordinary days in June where birth and awakening merge together into some kind of happiness. There's a sense of peace, yet still a sense of purpose.

"Okay, Michael," I thought. "What if you do get into college? What will you study? What do you want to be?" I looked at the choppy water topped off by the whitecaps, and in the sky small, fair-weather clouds were just beginning to form. And then it hit me: "Schmuck! You've got to be a teacher!" Then just as suddenly, "But what about being an artist?" Then I realized something that I guess I always knew: I could draw nicely, but I would never be a great artist. The thought of being a commercial artist may have been fun when I was younger, but it no longer appealed to me. Teaching, on the other hand, was something that I knew I enjoyed and something I knew I could do well. It seems my whole navy experience was designed to lead me in that direction. I thought about Major Dumont and how he had taught me that being a man was more than just fighting in combat; a "man" was someone who took responsibility for himself and all his actions. I guess he made me realize what the Yiddish expression "be a mensch" really meant.

I thought of the other folks I had met who led me to the realization that I should become a teacher. Billy Pierce showed me, among many other things, that being with little kids could be fun and rewarding when you taught them something they wanted to learn—even if it was just a tune on the piano. And then there was my striker Bobby Jonson, who was my first real student. He taught me that having people just memorize information wasn't teaching—that learning was much more than parroting back memorized phrases. Steve Schroeder made that even clearer to me when he explained that information, or intelligence, was what you needed to get started, but it was using the intelligence you had gathered to solve problems and make decisions that made you smart. That was what education should be about.

The subtler aspects of education, like morality and justice, were long ago established by my family's religious and ethnic roots. The need to be good, to be educated, and to be responsible to others was important, as was the need to defend what you believed in no matter what the consequences would be. It was Homer who taught me that other cultures could have the same goals for a world without prejudice. They too needed acceptance and understanding, only their needs frequently had to be obtained through ways that the social and political realities of the times dictated. And it was a ghost, Charlie, who taught me the importance of believing in things that were not always of this Earth. He showed me the importance of mystery in life—that some things should not always be explainable.

The women I met, like Rosie and Sister Marie Therese, also taught me lessons that would make me a better teacher. Sister Marie showed me that people representing institutional authority were also human. When I became a teacher, I would make sure that my students knew that I laughed and cried, went to movies, and even shopped at the same stores they did. Rosie made it clear that being an adult meant that men and women were partners; both were responsible to each other for dealing with strong, and sometimes seemingly uncontrollable, sexual desires. These lessons needed to be learned, and we shouldn't be afraid to embrace them. My friend and mentor Anne Baxter was my role model for my future career. She taught me that one teaches through guidance and discovery, not by rigid rules of authority and positions of power.

I guess I already knew that I was meant to be a teacher. Going to college and actually becoming one would be the culmination of my family's hopes and my own need to do what I was now certain I was meant to do. I thought of that line from Lowell's poem again: "Everything is upward striving." I watched the whitecaps form, and as I rubbed up on the stubble of my beard I smiled, remembered old Black Tooth, and thought, "there's hope for us all."

978-0-595-43323-0
0-595-43323-5